James W. Benson

Time and Time-Tellers

by James W. Benson

James W. Benson

Time and Time-Tellers
by James W. Benson

ISBN/EAN: 9783337362850

Printed in Europe, USA, Canada, Australia, Japan

Cover: Foto ©Andreas Hilbeck / pixelio.de

More available books at **www.hansebooks.com**

TIME AND TIME-TELLERS.

BY

JAMES W. BENSON.

LONDON:

ROBERT HARDWICKE, 192, PICCADILLY.

1875.

INDEX TO THE ILLUSTRATIONS.

MODERN WATCHES.

ESCAPEMENTS TO WATCHES.

BALANCES, ETC.

CLOCK ESCAPEMENTS.

TIME AND TIME-TELLERS.

TIME cannot be thoroughly defined, nor even properly comprehended by mankind, for our personal acquaintance with it is so brief that our longest term is compared to a span, and to 'the grass which in the morning is green and groweth up, and in the evening is cut down and withered.' The ordinary thinker can scarcely carry his idea of Time beyond that small portion of it which he has known, under the name of life-time. The metaphysician classes Time with those other mysteries,—Space, Matter, Motion, Force, Consciousness, which are the Gordian knots of Mental Science. Time is naturally divided into three most unequal parts,—whereof the Past includes all that has happened until now from that far-distant period when 'Heaven and Earth rose out of chaos;' the Present is but a moment, expended in a breath, to be again like that breath momentarily renewed; the Future is, as the Past,—'a wide unbounded pros-

1

pect,' an 'undiscovered country,' into which Prophecy
itself penetrates but partially, and even then bears back
to us but small information; for its language catches
the character of a grander clime, and the denizens
of this lower earth are incapable of understanding
its gorgeous metaphors; the brightness is as blinding
as the darkness. We may attempt to pierce the
Future by the light which History throws from the
Past, but History's record is imperfect; her chronicles
are of the rudest and most unreliable character;
her most valued memorials serve but to make Past
'darkness visible,' her most ancient registers reach
back but a short distance compared with those testi-
monies which geologists have discovered, and given
us veritable 'sermons in stones' about. The Past is,
indeed, scarcely less of a mystery than the Future; even
the Present we only know in part, but we do know
that the brief term during which man 'flits across the
stage' of time ere he goes hence and is no more seen,
is of inestimable value. Most of us soon make the
discovery that the world has much to teach which
there is little time to learn and still less time to apply
to good purpose. *Ars longa, vita brevis est,* is the general expression of human experience. For every man
there are duties and labours for which time is all too
short; just as he begins to understand and to perform his work wisely and successfully, the 'spirit of
the destinies,' as Mr Carlyle would say, 'calls him

away;' but whither he goeth is as great a mystery as
whence he cometh. This, however, we do know, no-
wise man ever disregarded Time, inasmuch as of this
treasure there is no laying in a fresh store when life's
supply has been exhausted; the wasters, the 'killers'
of Time, like the foolish virgins who neglected their
lamps, are met invariably with the 'Not so,'—as the
door of opportunity is shut in their faces. Like the
dial with the inscription ' Nulla vestigia retrorsum'
each man's steps are taken never to be retraced, the
act once done can no more be recalled than the
shadow on the dial can go backward. What wonder
then that the most thoughtful of men are particularly
careful of their time, regulating their use of it with
the utmost precision and weighing it out as scrupul-
ously as a miser would his gold? What wonder that
they should sigh and grieve over a wasted day, and
with bitter self-reproach should say to themselves as
Titus did, ' Perdidi diem,'—I have lost a day? What
wonder is it that such should teach themselves to
wrestle with Time, even as Jacob wrestled with the
angel, for a blessing; and to regard those reckless
ones, in whose butterfly existence are counted only
the 'shining hours,'—as the bee might be supposed
to regard the idle gnats which frolic in the sun-
beams heedless both of to-day and of to-morrow.

The poets are our best interpreters of Time, and
they seem never tired of referring to it and symbol-

ising it by every possible figure, emblem, and trope.* Celerity of motion and brevity of duration are discovered to be its chief characteristics.   Time is therefore depicted as flying,—fast, noiselessly, and uninterruptedly.   It is a river, speeding on with imperceptible but resistless pace to the ocean of eternity. It is a stern vigorous old man—Time is already old —rushing by us with never-slackening strides, bearing blessings for each and all, but we must be upon the alert to strive with him for his gifts—'to seize Time by the forelock'—or he will forget to bestow them.

We too often charge upon Time the evil which is the result of our own lack of energy, and thus it happens that although in kindly moments our poets seem to delight in exalting and glorifying him for all manner of enjoyments, at others they can find no word too coarse or uncivil to apply to him.   'Time,' says Shakspeare, 'is a very bankrupt,' adding,

> 'Nay, he's a thief too ; have you not heard men say
> That time comes stealing on by night and day?'

Time is, in proverbial philosophy, the most churlish and unaccommodating of acquaintances,—'Time and tide tarry for no man.'   Time is always liable to be chided, as we have said, when one feels like Ham-

* Phœbus Apollo in Ovid's Metamorphoses claims that he is Time's special exponent :—

> ———— 'Per me, quod eritque, fuitque,
> Estque, patet ; per me concordant carmina nervis.'

let, 'The times are out of joint;' although our next-
door neighbour may, with as much or more reason, be
blessing the self-same hour we are condemning.
Time is indeed all things to all men, and 'travels
divers paces with divers persons.' Sweet Rosa-
lind described long ago 'who Time ambles withal,
who Time trots withal, and who he stands still
withal.' 'I prithee,' asks Orlando, 'who doth he trot
withal?' and no matter how often we overhear her
reply, we shall listen with delight to the quaint language of the pretty rejoinder,—'Marry, he trots hard
with a young maid between the contract of her mar-
riage and the day it is solemnized; if the interim be
but a se'nnight, Time's pace is so hard that it seems
the length of seven years.' 'And who ambles Time
withal?' 'With a priest that lacks Latin and a rich
man that hath not the gout; for the one sleeps easily
because he cannot study; and the other lives merrily
because he feels no pain; the one lacking the burthen
of lean and wasteful learning, the other knowing no
burthen of heavy tedious penury. These ambles
Time withal.' 'Who doth he gallop withal?'
'With a thief to the gallows; for though he go as
softly as foot can fall, he thinks himself too soon
there.' 'Who stays Time still withal?' 'With
lawyers in the vacation; for they sleep between term
and term, and then they perceive not how Time
wags.'

If Roger Bacon's Brazen-head could have repeated and continued his oracular utterances at fixed intervals he would have been a very sensational performer over some prominent public time-piece of the present day. If only once in twelve months, say at midnight, when the year ends, he could have pronounced his three important speeches, 'Time is;—Time was;—Time's past!' he might have rivalled some of our best actors or orators in attracting the multitude; unfortunately, however, our mechanical clockwork performers have never risen to the dignity of speech, and the secret of Friar Bacon's magic died with the inventor of gunpowder,—which last it is a pity, perhaps, did not also slip out of use and memory along with it. 'Time is, time was, time's past' seems to comprise a whole world of hopes, fears, and lost opportunities, and sounds like a little condensed history of all that ever has happened or ever can happen. Herein we may imagine we can observe the wonder-working qualities of Time, solving all mysteries, bringing everything whether of good or evil to fruition, testing friendship and love, solacing troubled and wounded hearts, and healing all manner of griefs; but then we also remark that he is the abaser of the proud as well as the uplifter of the humble. If he builds, he as surely destroys, being, indeed, the Great Spoiler, *edax rerum*, before whose breath myriads of living things through all generations have faded away, in regular sequence, and towns and cities and the several civilizations of the world have one after another decayed and perished with all their wondrous works, and glories, and aspirations.

'Who shall contend with Time—unvanquished Time,
The conqueror of conquerors, and lord
Of desolation?'

Time's chronicle is of itself proof of his character, for the very record of his deeds he does not permit to be of long endurance. Time was, before the earliest historian began to take note of him, before the 'twilight of fable,' and before the most primitive symbol. Time himself were too brief to tell of his various experiences, the full value and purport of which we shall never know, until we have bridged the abyss which separates the present from the future. Time and the world, we are told, commenced life simultaneously, and their twin birth was greeted triumphantly 'with the music of the spheres,' the morning stars sang together rejoicingly; and it is also said that their courses shall be simultaneously determined when the edict shall be promulgated that 'Time shall be no more.' When will that great event take place? is a question which has occupied the attention of many theologians and others, who temporarily forget that 'of that day and hour knoweth no man.' As of the end so of the beginning of Time, there is to us no landmark, though geologists are endeavouring to prove that they have

traced some of his earliest footprints in this world of
ours. Professor Tyndall tells us that 'not for six
thousand, nor for sixty thousand, nor for six thousand
thousand, but for æons, embracing untold millions of
years, this earth has been the theatre of life and death.
The riddle of the rocks has been read by the geologist
and palæontologist, from subcambrian depths to the
deposits thickening over the sea-bottoms of to-day.
And upon the leaves of that stone book are stamped
the characters, plainer and surer than those formed by
the ink of history, which carry the mind back into
abysses of past time compared with which six thousand years cease to have a visual angle.'

Although Time is so vast in his operations and so
truly marvellous in his many features, it has, nevertheless, been found possible to measure his shorter intervals with the greatest accuracy,—even to but a
few seconds in a year. It took some centuries to
accomplish this feat, but it is now surely and sys-
tematically done. The stages of horological science
are some of them remote, but they are well worth
studying. The earliest divisions of time were doubt-
less those made by the operations of Nature, pro-
ducing day and night,—the sun and moon were the
earliest chronometers, and, marked by them, 'the evening and the morning were the first day.' It is even
now by noting the recurrence of certain celestial
phenomena that we are enabled to certify to ourselves

the accuracy of our time-pieces, but although the motion of the heavenly bodies is the standard of computation for lengthened periods, it is found more convenient to reckon short terms, such as seconds, minutes, and hours, by machinery set in motion by a spring or by weights mathematically adjusted, and this in a word has given birth to the science called Horology.

We can readily comprehend the division of time into days and nights, for these, as we have said, are the natural divisions. Let us trace the origin of more arbitrary periods, such as hours, and weeks, and months, and years. First, then, as to days, let it be remembered that the beginning and ending of an ordinary English day differs in several respects from those of other nations. The Jews reckon their day, as do also the Greeks and Italians, from sunset to sunset; the Persians from sunrise to sunrise. The astronomical and nautical day is computed from noon to noon, and is reckoned by 24 hours, not by twice 12,—as, for instance, instead of writing half-past four in the morning of, we will say, Jan. 2, the astronomer would write Jan. 1. 16 h. 30 m. Our ordinary English day is reckoned from 12 to 12 at midnight, after the fashion set by Ptolemy, which has this advantage over the method of reckoning from sunrise or sunset, that the latter periods are continually varying with the seasons of the year. The grouping of seven days into a week is shown in Genesis, but the seventh day is there alone specially named. The Sabbath is still kept by the Jews on the seventh day, but Christians keep the first day of the week in honour of Christ's resurrection, and call it the Lord's Day. After the older planetary method, Sunday was named in honour of the Sun, Monday of the Moon, Tuesday of Tuesco, or Mars, Wednesday of Woden or Mercury, Thursday of Thor, Friday of Friga, Venus, Saturday of Saturn. The Month, named after the Moon in consequence of a month being nearly equal to the time occupied by the Moon in going through all her changes, is again classed under the names lunar or calendar; the lunar month is rather more than 29½ days, but as the solar month is nearly a day longer it would require more than twelve lunar months to make a year, arbitrary additions have been therefore made to each month, some consisting of 30, some of 31 days; and months so arranged to form the calendar are called calendar months, twelve of which make a year of about 365¼ days. Until the time of Julius Cæsar the year was reckoned as of 365 days only, a number which after many centuries required the addition of ninety days to rectify, he therefore ordered one of the years to consist of 444 days, and that subsequently every fourth year should contain 366 days. Even this very summary imperial method was attended with its drawbacks and difficulties, for the

earth's revolution round the Sun is made in eleven
minutes eleven seconds, less than 365¼ days, which
minutes in the course of about 1600 years required to
be taken into consideration, and in 1582 Pope Gregory XIII. took off ten days by making the 5th of
October the 15th ; but the Gregorian time was not
introduced into England till 1752 when the error
amounted to about eleven, so eleven days were subtracted from 1752 leaving it only 354 days,—much to
the indignation of the illiterate people of that time,
who clamoured, assembled in great mobs to testify to
their sense of the great injury inflicted upon them,
'Give us back our Eleven days,'—one of Hogarth's
prints of the 'Election' exhibits a paper containing
this very inscription. The fury of the populace at
being robbed of its precious time availed not; the day
after the 2nd of September, 1752, was made the 14th
of September, and from that time dated the New
Style, since which the year has been almost exactly
correct. Up to 1752 the legal year began in England
on the 25th of March, and it was usual up to that
day to employ two dates, as 1750-1 ; but since the
change of style the year has commenced with the first
of January,—nearly midwinter. As there is one day
more than fifty-two weeks in a year every year begins
one day later in the week than the preceding year;
and after leap-year two days later. The only country
in Europe which still retains the Old Style is Russia,

—the difference between the styles, now twelve days,
is usually indicated by O. S. and N. S., or as in
one or two of our watch illustrations by 'Russian'
and 'Gregorian.' As regards the smaller divisions of
time, it should be noted that the minute and the hour
are thus reckoned,—the Earth divided into 360 degrees, turning upon its axis once every twenty-four
hours, brings fifteen degrees under the sun each hour,
and makes those fifteen degrees of longitude equivalent to one hour of time,—fifteen geographical miles
being equivalent to one minute of time.

The earliest horologe or hour measurer of which
history makes mention is that called the *Polos*, and
the *Gnomon*. Herodotus (lib. II.) ascribes their invention to the Babylonians, but Phavorinus claims it
for Anaximander, and Pliny for Anaximenes. The
Gnomon, which was the more simple and probably the
more ancient instrument, consisted simply of a staff
or pillar fixed perpendicularly in a sunny place, the
shadow of which was measured by feet upon the place
where it fell,—the flight of time being computed
thereby. In later times the word *Gnomon* was the
title of the sun-dial, and it is the name still in use for
the style or finger which throws the shadow on the
dial and thus indicates the hour. The *Polos* or *Helio-
tropion* was no doubt a superior instrument to the
earliest *Gnomon*, but, from its being so seldom mentioned, we may suppose it not to have been so gener-

ally used. The *Polos* consisted of a basin, in the middle of which the perpendicular staff or finger was erected, and marked by lines the twelve portions of the day. The *Dial* was but another form of *Polos;* its name indicates a Roman origin,—namely, from *Dies*, a day, but there was a Greek sun-dial called *Sciathericum*, from *skia*, a shadow. The invention is said to have been derived by the Jews from the Babylonians, to whom, as we have seen, Herodotus ascribed it, and there is mention made in the xxxviii. of Isaiah of the dial of Ahaz,—a king who began to reign 741 B.C. The form of the Dial of Ahaz has not been ascertained; but there is reason to believe that the ancient Jews and the Brahmins were acquainted with the uses of the dial and applied it to astronomical purposes. Dials were, it is said, not known in Rome before 293 B.C., when one was set up by Papirius Cursor the Roman General, near the Temple of Quirinus. At Athens there is an octagonal temple of the Winds still standing, which shows on each side the lines of a vertical dial and the centres where the *Gnomons* were placed. At one time the art of Dialling was most assiduously studied; its rudiments may be described as follows:

The plane of every dial represents the plane of some great circle on the earth, and the *Gnomon* the earth's axis; the vertex of a right *Gnomon*, the centre of the earth or visible heavens. The earth itself, com-

pared with its distance from the sun, is considered as a
point, and therefore if a small sphere of glass be placed
upon any part of the earth's surface so that its axis be
parallel to the axis of the earth, and the sphere have
such lines upon it, and such plans within it, as above
described, it will show the hour of the day as truly as if
it were placed at the earth's centre, and the shell of
the earth were as transparent as glass.   The diversity
of the titles of sun-dials arises from the different
situation of the planes, and the different figure of the
surfaces whereon they are described, whence they are
denominated equinoctial, horizontal, vertical, polar,
erect, direct, declining, inclining, reclining, cylindrical, &c.

The Pocket Ring Dial.

All the before-mentioned time-measurers were up
to a certain period non-portable, and in addition to

the drawback of being unserviceable excepting when
the weather was clear and the days bright were
as useless for private purposes, as they were un-
adapted for the winter-time or for night.   The next
step was therefore a portable dial, but this was probably not invented until after a very long interval.
The Dial of which the above is an illustration, was
probably one of the earliest of portable time-keepers,
the time being shown by means of a hole through
which the light fell on the inside, which had an inner
ring adaptable to the day and the month.   Ring-dials
of this description were in common use within the last
century in this country, and were manufactured in
large numbers at Sheffield when watches were too ex-
pensive to be generally attainable.   Some of these
Dial-rings were of superior construction, and were
made by means of more than one ring to serve for
different latitudes.   As an example of a still greater
advance in the manufacture of pocket dials, see the
illustration on the next page.

The Dial consists of a thin silver plate properly
divided and marked, and having a compass with glass
cover sunk at one end of it.   The *Gnomon* or style
moves upon a hinge so as to allow of its lying flat
upon the Dial while in the pocket, and thus rendering
the instrument conveniently portable.   The *Gnomon*
itself is also susceptible of elevation or depression and
the beak of the bird carved on a thin slip of silver at

its side marks the exact extent of the *Gnomon's* elevation.   This Dial is indubitably of French manufacture.

One would imagine that it was such a dial as this
that Shakspeare had in his mind's eye when he wrote
the well-known passage which he put into the mouth

Silver Pocket Dial (in the collection of the Honble Company of
Clockmakers, London).

of Jaques, wherein that philosophic satirist describes
his meeting with a fool in the forest.

> ' Good morrow, fool, quoth I.   " No sir," quoth he,
> " Call me not fool till heaven hath sent me fortune ;
> And then he drew *a dial from his poke*,
> And looking on it with lack-lustre eye,

Says, very wisely, " It is ten o'clock :
Thus we may see," quoth he, " how the world wags :
'Tis but an hour ago since it was nine,
And after one hour more 'twill be eleven.
And so from hour to hour we ripe and ripe,
And then from hour to hour we rot and rot.
And thereby hangs a tale." When I did hear
The motley fool thus moral on the time,
My lungs began to crow like Chanticleer,
That fools should be so deep contemplative ;
And I did laugh, sans intermission,
An hour by his dial.'

What the fool's dial was, has given rise to many
conjectures, but there is no better authority perhaps
on the subject than Mr Halliwell, from whose magni-
ficent and elaborate folio we will make the following
very interesting extract.

'The term dial appears to have been applied in
Shakspeare's time to anything for measuring time in
which the hours were marked, so that the allusion
here may be either to a watch, or to a portable journey
ring, or small dial. The expression "it is ten o'clock "
is not decisive, as it may be considered to be used
merely in the sense of the hour thus named. * * A
watch even is sometimes called a clock, * * * and it
seems by no means unlikely that the common ring
dial which has been in use for several centuries up to
a comparatively recent period, should be the dial referred to in the text.'

Whatever may have been the shape of the dial

2

which Jaques saw drawn from the fool's 'poke,' it is
an undoubted fact that portable dials did serve the
part of time-keepers, and were in their way valuable
as such to those who had learnt how to use them.
But the dial would not do the work of the watch in
an age when people no longer travel by the waggon-
load or with pack-horse, but are whirled fifty or sixty
miles in that time and have to reckon their engagements
not by the day, but by the minute. The world no
longer 'wags' in jog-trot style, but speeds at steam-
pressure and sends its messages by lightning-conduct-
or; it consequently values its time more highly and
measures it more carefully.

The Horologe which possibly next succeeded in
date the invention of the Dial, was the Clepsydra or
Water-Clock, the precise antiquity of which is however unknown.

The CLEPSYDRA is so named because the water
escapes from it as it were by stealth, but in a regulated
flow so as to permit of the lapse of time being computed thereby, even as by sand running through
sand-glasses. The Clepsydra appears to have been
at first used to limit the time during which persons
were allowed to speak in the Athenian Courts of
Justice; 'the first water,' says Æschines, 'being
given to the accuser, the second to the accused,
and the third to the judges,'—a special officer being
appointed in the courts for the purpose of watching

the Clepsydra and stopping it when any documents
were read whereby the speaker was interrupted.

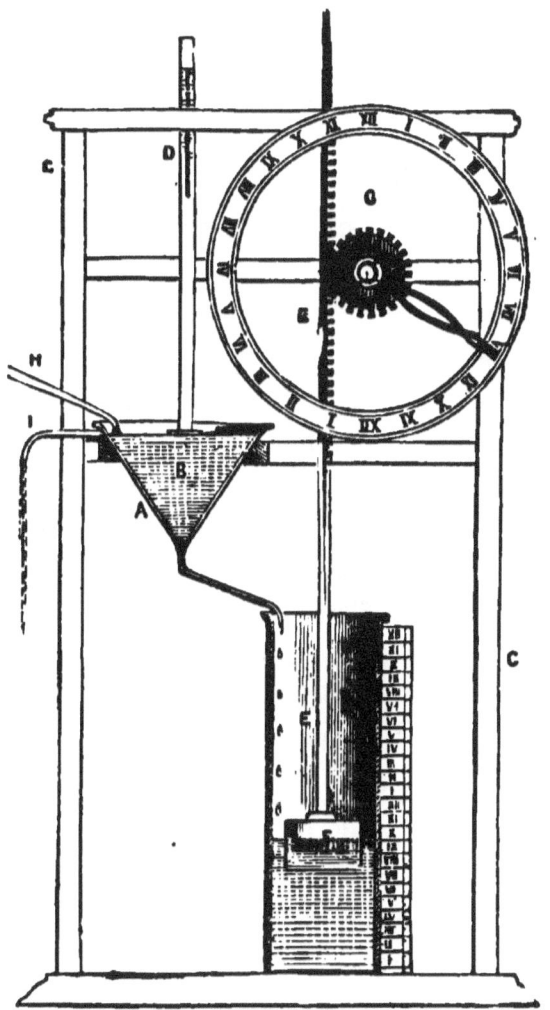

The Clepsydra, or Water-Clock of the Greeks.

The time, and consequently the water allowed, de-

pended upon the importance of the case. This
custom, says Phavorinus, was to prevent babbling,
that such as spake should be brief in their speeches.
Ctesibius of Alexandria, who lived about 245, invented
a much improved water-clock, mentioned by Vitruvius
and Athenæus. Another kind of Clepsydra consisted
of a vessel of water having a hole in it through which
the fluid gradually escaped; a miniature boat floated
upon the water and descended as the water decreased,
whilst an oar placed in the boat indicated the hour
by pointing to certain line-marks on the side of the
vessel. The hole through which the water dropped
was made, we are told, through a pearl, because it was
supposed that the action of the water upon the pearl
would not, as upon other substances, enlarge the aper-
ture, nor would the pearl, it was imagined, be choked
by the adhesion of any other material. The chief
fault of the Clepsydra as a chronometer arose from
the inequality of the flow of water, it being found to
escape more rapidly when the vessel was full than
when it was becoming empty, and also more speedily
in hot weather than in cold. The Egyptians are
however said to have measured by this machine the
course of the sun; by it Tycho-Brahe computed the
motion of the stars; and by it Dudley made his
maritime observations. Plato furnished the original
idea of the hydraulic organ by inventing a Clepsydra,
or water-clock, which played upon flutes the hours of

the night when darkness precluded their being shown by the index. Clepsydræ are still used in India.

The SAND-GLASS, as we have said, is an instrument of the same character as the Clepsydra,—the one measuring time by the fall of water and the other by the running of sand. Sand-glasses are known to have been used 200 B.C. The best hour-glasses, it is said, were those in which powdered egg-shells well dried in the oven were used instead of sand, such powder being less affected by changes in the atmosphere than sand would be. Sand-glasses are now seldom used except on board ship, and by domestics to compute the time for the boiling of eggs.

King Alfred's invention for measuring time by the burning of candles, which were marked by circular lines to show the progress of the hours, was another effort of rude skill, which however could have been but partially successful even in the opinion of its inventor, for the accuracy of candle-horologes is interfered with by many different influences, prominent among which must of course have been the varying qualities of the materials used in their manufacture, and the more or less care with which they were guarded from the wind, so as to prevent their guttering.

We now come to consider the date of the next grand step in the progress of Horology,—namely, that of the invention of the *clock*. The name itself may be derived either from the French, *la cloche*, a bell, or from the German, *die gloke*, or *die kloke*. There is no doubt that the word *cloche* was meant to distinguish the instrument which marked the hours by sounding a bell, from the *montre* or watch, which (derived from the Latin *monstro*, to show) merely shows the time by its hands. In ancient books the word *cloche* simply stands for a bell,—the monks being accustomed to ring a bell at certain periods marked for them by their sun-dials or hour-glasses, and ' What's o'clock ? ' in old writers is often merely equivalent to the inquiry, ' What hour was last struck by bell ? ' The word horologe or hour-measurer of course equally applied to the sun-dial, the clepsydra, and the clock, and this convertibility of terms makes it all the more difficult to trace the point at which the newer invention began. Beckmann, in an ingenious analysis of various statements as to the first inventors of clocks made to go by weights and wheels, ascribes the invention to the eleventh century, but he does not attempt to name the first clock-maker. His authority for the date is the life of William Abbot of Hirshan, wherein there is mention made of a machine used by the monks for measuring time, which cannot in Beckmann's opinion have been a clepsydra. Beckmann does not believe that clocks were of European origin, but that they were derived from the Saracens. He founds his opinion upon a horologe described by Trithenius

which was presented by the Sultan of Egypt in 1232,
to the Emperor Frederic II. of Germany. 'In the
same year,' says he, ' the Saladin of Egypt sent by his
ambassadors, as a gift to Frederic II., a valuable
machine of wonderful construction, worth more than
5000 ducats. For it appeared to resemble internally
a celestial globe in which figures of the sun, moon,
and other planets, formed with the greatest skill,
moved, being impelled by weights and wheels, so that
performing their course in certain and fixed intervals,
they pointed out the hour, night and day, with infal-
lible certainty; also the twelve signs of the Zodiac
with appropriate characters, moved with the firma-
ment, contained within themselves the course of the
planet.'

To whom the high honour belongs of inventing
the clock is, to use a not unknown phrase, ' lost in
the mists of antiquity.' All the ancients who were
reported as skilful in mechanics seem to have obtained
a modicum of credit as clock-inventors. Archimedes
and Posidonius before the Christian era, Boëthius in
the 5th century, Pacificus about the middle of the 9th,
Gerbert at the end of the 10th, Wallingford near the
beginning of the 14th, and Dondi at the end of the
14th, have each in their turn been asserted to be the
inventors of the clock.

The sphere of Archimedes, made 200 B.C., as
mentioned by Claudian, was evidently an instrument

with a maintaining power but without a regulator, and therefore would not measure time in any other manner than as a planetarium, turned by a handle, measures, or rather exhibits, the respective velocities of the heavenly bodies; and the same may be said of the sphere of Posidonius, as mentioned by Cicero ('De naturâ Deorum'). The clock of Boëthius was a clepsydra, as was also that of Pacificus, according to some, for Bailly in his History of Modern Astronomy asserts that Pacificus was the inventor of a clock going by means of a weight and a balance, and if so the invention must be ascribed to Pacificus; but Bailly gives no authority for his assertion. Gerbert's horologe is said to have been merely a sun-dial, and Wallingford's horologe, called the Albion, must have as much resembled a planetarium as a clock, for the motions of all the heavenly bodies appear to have been conducted by the maintaining power, whatever that was, without controlling mechanism. This instrument, made in 1326, is also described as having shown the ebb and flow of the sea, the hours, and the minutes.

There are, however, still earlier data as to clocks in England than this of Wallingford's, for we find that in 1288 a stone clock-tower was erected opposite Westminster Hall with a clock which cost 800 marks, the proceeds of a fine imposed upon Ralph de Hengham, Chief Justice of the Queen's Bench. The tower mentioned was still standing in 1715, and in it

was a clock which struck the great bell known as Tom
of Westminster so as to be heard by the people in all
the law courts.   In Queen Elizabeth's time the clock
was changed for a dial upon the clock tower, which,
however, bore upon its face the same Virgilian
motto, 'Discite justitiam moniti,'—referring to the
fine inflicted upon the Chief Justice for making an
alteration in a record by which a poor dependent was
made to pay 13*s*. 4*d*. instead of 6*s*. 8*d*.   A dial with
this motto was still to be seen in Palace Yard, Westminster, within the last dozen years, but was removed
with the houses which were then demolished to make
way for the gilded palings which have since been
erected between Palace Yard and Bridge Street,
Westminster.

In 1292 a clock was placed in Canterbury Cathedral, which, according to a statement in a Cottonian
MS., cost £30, a large sum at that time.

Dante, who died in 1321, aged 57, makes the
earliest mention of an *orologio* which struck the hour:

'Indi come orologio che *ne chiami*
Nel hora che la sposa, d'Idio surge
Amattinar lo sposo, perche l'ami.'
Il Paradiso.—C. X.

In 1344 James Dondi constructed at Padua, by the
command of Hubert, prince of Carrara, a clock
similar to Wallingford's, and thus obtained for himself
the title of *Horologius*, which, it is said, is still borne

by his descendants in Florence. In 1364 Henry de
Wyck, a German, made a clock for Charles V. of
France, which was erected in the tower of his palace.
This clock was regulated by a balance, the teeth of
the crown-wheel acted upon two small levers called
pallets which projected from, and formed part of, an
upright spindle or staff, on which was fixed the balance,
and the clock was regulated by shifting the weights
placed at each end of the balance.

In 1368 Edward granted protection against 'injuri-
am, molestiam, violentiam, damnum, aut gravamen'
to three Dutch horologers, John and William Une-
man and John Lietuyt, who had been invited to this
country from Delft.

Chaucer, who died in 1400, speaks of a cock
crowing with such regularity as to rival a clock:

> ' Full sikerer (surer) was his crowing in his loge
>   As is a clok, or any abbey orloge.'

Whether the abbey horologe referred to was really
a clock in our sense of the term, or merely the bell
rung by the monks at a certain hour indicated by the
clepsydra, is matter of conjecture, but the probability
is, that clockmaking had advanced sufficiently about
this time to have given rise to Chaucer's simile.
Froissart speaks of a famous clock which struck the
hours, and was remarkable for its mechanism, and
which was removed in 1332 by Philip the Hardy, duke

of Burgundy, from Courtrai to his capital at Dijon.

After this date frequent mention is made of clocks in various histories, some of which instruments remain even to the present day. Dr Heylin thus describes a famous clock and dial in the Cathedral of Lunden in Denmark. 'In the dial are to be seen distinctly the year, month, week, day, and every hour of the day throughout the year, with the feasts, both those which are movable and fixed, together with the motions of the sun and moon, and their passage through each degree of the zodiac. Then for the clock, it is so framed by artificial engines that whensoever it is to strike, two horsemen encounter one another, giving as many blows apiece as the bell sounds hours, and on the opening of a door there appeareth a theatre, the Virgin Mary on a throne with Christ in her arms, and the three kings or Magi (with their several trains) marching in order, doing humble reverence, and presenting severally their gifts,—two trumpeters sounding all the while, to adorn the pomp of the procession.'

The clock at Hampton Court is one of the most ancient in England, but all that remains of the original structure is the dial and work connected with it, facing the east, in the second court of the old part of the building erected by Wolsey. Of the ancient body or works there is no record, and its maker is unknown, but it bears the initials N. O. and the date 1540.

There is a celebrated antique clock at Strasburg which is described as striking the quarter-hours by four figures, symbols of the ages of man ;—the first being struck by a child with an apple, the second by a youth with an arrow, the third by a man with a staff, and the fourth by an old man with a crutch, then came Death, who struck the hour, and thus reminded the observer that his last hour would eventually arrive.

From the evidence adduced respecting the origin and inventors of the clock it is not unreasonable to conclude with Ferdinand Berthoud (a Frenchman who wrote much and was a great authority upon the subject) that such a clock as that which was constructed by Henry de Wyck for Charles the Wise of France, was not the invention of one man, but was the result of a series of inventions made at different times by various persons, each of which is worthy to be considered a separate invention. It was the simple employment of the natural force of gravity as to the fall of bodies in free space, that paved the way to the extreme accuracy and constancy of rate which belong to the clocks of modern times, and the conclusion to which Mons. Berthoud arrived respecting the progression of the essential improvements is thus stated :—

1. Toothed wheel-work was known in ancient times, and particularly to Archimedes, whose instru-

ment was provided with a maintaining power, but had no regulator or controlling mechanism.

2. The weight applied as a maintainer at first had a fly, most probably similar to that of a kitchen-jack.

3. The ratchet-wheel and click for winding up the weight, without detaching the teeth of the great wheel.

4. The regulation of the fly depending upon the state of the air, it was abandoned, and a balance substituted.

5. An escapement next became indispensable, as constituting with the balance a more regular check than a fly upon the tendency which a falling weight has to accelerate its velocity.

6. The application of a dial-plate and hand to indicate the hours was a consequence of the regularity introduced into the going part.

7. The striking portion, to proclaim at a distance, without the aid of a watcher, the hour that was indicated : and this was followed by the alarum.

8. The reduction and accommodation of all this bulky machinery to a portable and compact size, as in watches.

Such a succession of ingenious contrivances, introduced by different men to improve upon the first rude instrument, is perfectly analogous to the successive improvements which have been made in the modern clock, since that of Henry de Wyck's was

constructed. Large iron wheels, continually exposed
to the oxidizing influence of the air, in which unequal
and ill-shapen teeth were cut with the inaccuracy of
a manual operation, were by no means calculated to
transmit the maintaining power with perfect regularity
to the balance, supposing it to have been a good regulator; but when it is further remembered that the
alternate direct pushes of the escape-wheel against
the pallets must have produced jerks, and destroyed,
or greatly disturbed, the regularity of this most essential part of the mechanism, great accuracy was not to
be expected; even minutes were deemed too small
portions of time to be shown by such a machine.
The clock was set daily by some person specially
appointed to the office, and even then was not to be
depended upon, for forty minutes' variation in twenty-
four hours was not thought to be an ill performance.

The most ancient clocks had no pendulum such
as we now see, but had instead a balance vibrating
on the top of the clock, as seen in illustration, p. 108,
which is an example of ancient clock-work.

Upon the invention of springs, in lieu of weights,
as the maintaining or motive power in clocks, which
was made towards the close of the fifteenth century,
it became obvious that time-pieces might be rendered
portable, and that the new motive power, a coiled
spring, could act independently of position. This discovery was of great importance, and yet to whom we

are indebted for it is unknown; the value of the invention became still more apparent when the fusee, or mechanism for equalizing the variable power of a coiled spring, was applied. Berthoud says, ' It was soon perceived that the action of the spring being much greater at the height of its tension than at the end, great variations in the watch resulted therefrom. This was remedied by a mechanism called *stack-freed*, that is, a kind of curve, by means of which the great spring of the barrel acted on a straight spring, which opposed itself to its action, and when this spring was nearly down, acted more feebly.' The word *stack-freed* was stated to be German, and therefore gave rise to a supposition that the invention was of German origin, but the word is not to be found in a German dictionary, and, if ever German, it was probably strictly technical, and soon became obsolete. Berthoud has given a drawing and description of a portable clock, probably by Jourdain, without a fusee, and some of the modern continental watchmakers have, perhaps, derived their idea from it of making a watch keep time without a fusee. Up to the close of the 15th century the motive power in clocks was always obtained by means of weights; the invention of the coiled spring rendered them portable.

Whatever be the date or origin of the watch or portable clock, certain it is that there was mention made of such an instrument as far back as 1494, by

Gaspar Visconti, an Italian poet, who in a sonnet describes 'Certain small and portable clocks made with a little ingenuity, and which are continually going, showing the hours, many courses of the planets, the festivals, and striking when the time requires it.' The sonnet is, as it were, composed by a person in love, who compares himself to one of these clocks. One of the earliest places of watch manufacture was Nuremberg, and foremost among its horologers was Peter Hele, who was thus described by Doppelmayer in his 'History of the Mathematicians and Artists of Nuremberg.'

'Peter Hele, a clockmaker, was everywhere esteemed a great artist on account of the pocket-clocks, which, soon after the year 1500, he first made in Nuremberg, with small wheels of steel. The invention, which with great justice may be ascribed to him, being something new, was praised by almost every one, even by the mathematicians of the time, with great admiration. He died 1540. On this subject Johannes Cocclæus, in his Commentary on the Cosmographia of Pomponius Mela, published in Nuremberg in 1511, makes the following announcement:—" Inveniuntur in dies subtiliora, etenim Petrus Hele, juvenis adhuc admodum, opera fecit, quæ doctissimi admirantur mathematici, nam ex ferro parva fabricat horologia, plurimis digesta rotulis, quæ, quocunque vertuntur, absque ullo pondere, et monstrant et pulsant XL.

horas.   Etiamsi in sinu, marsupiove contineantur." '
This quotation from Cocclæus may be thus translated :
—Ingenious things are just now being invented, for
Peter Hele, as yet but a young man, hath made works
which even the most learned mathematicians admire,
for he fabricates small horologes of iron fitted with
many wheels, which, whithersoever they are turned, and
without any weight, both show and strike forty hours,
—whether they be carried in the bosom or the pocket.

Doppelmayer in continuation says : ' This, already
so written by Cocclæus in 1511, shows in the clearest
way, that pocket-clocks were made at Nuremberg
many years ago, and he has fairly attributed the invention of them to this artist, since it was the most
deserving of admiration, and the newest of his time;
and which will be considered as a Nuremberg invention ; whence also clocks of this kind were for a long
time called Nuremberg living eggs,‾ because they at
first used to make them in the form of small eggs,
which name is to be found in the German translation
in chapter 26 of a strange book which F. Rabelais
has left behind him.   Hence it is evident how erro-
neous it is to ascribe, as many do, the invention of
small striking-clocks, as of these pocket-clocks, to
Isaac Habrecht, a well-known mathematician who
lived about the beginning of the last century, and
dwelt at Strasburg, whereas our Peter Hele had made
them in Nuremberg 100 years before.'

3

The art of watchmaking soon extended itself over
Europe, for we find that in France, in 1544, Francis
I. enacted a statute in favour of the corporation of
master clockmakers at Paris, to the effect that no one
should be permitted to make horologes unless he
should have been previously admitted into that
society. Of the most antique watches there are some
very interesting collections at the South Kensington
Museum and other places,—originally brought together by private persons whose antiquarian knowledge
has lit up the subject with wonderful interest. It would
be impossible to furnish in a volume such as this, a
regular series of such productions, showing the develop-
ment of artistic skill in the embellishment and design
of watches; we leave that duty to some future writer
who shall prepare an *edition de luxe*, and show therein,
in splendid colour-printing, all the beauties of ena-
melling on the precious metals, all the elegance, as
well as perhaps the oddity, of design, which are to be
observed in these highly-interesting works of art.
We will, for the nonce, be content with interspersing
our pages with a few examples, not perhaps of the
highest quality in point of design, but yet worthy of
notice, either as showing variety of form or as being
made valuable by historical associations. One of the
earliest specimens of very small watches which are
now extant is the one given on the next page.
     This little time-piece dates from the period

when blacksmiths were watchmakers, or at all events
when watchmakers were blacksmiths.   The works are
all of iron; the case was made, probably, before glass
was used for such instruments, and it is not unlikely
that this watch is of as old a shape as even the Nurem-

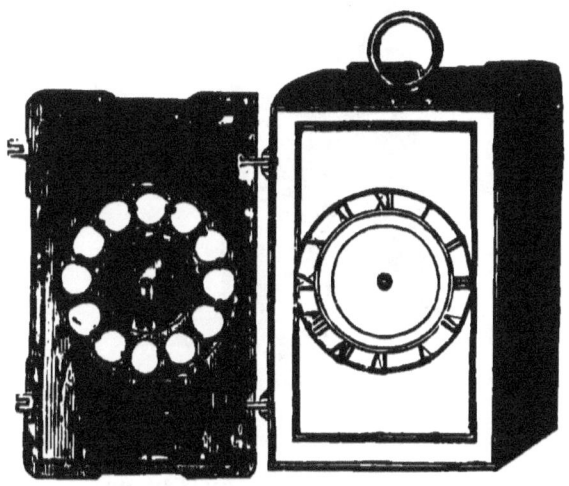

Ancient Watch, in form of a Book.

berg eggs.   A more ornamental time-piece, of perhaps
a somewhat later date, is the curious little instrument which is portrayed in our next illustration; the
works of which are also of iron.   It possesses the
advantage of serving either as a clock or a watch, or
as both, being of a portable size, and yet when set on a
stand would serve as a pretty ornament to a drawing-
room table.   The bell at the top is so arranged that
when the hand touches a trigger the hour is struck
upon it, but the bell itself may be detached without

any interference with the movement by which the
time is kept.

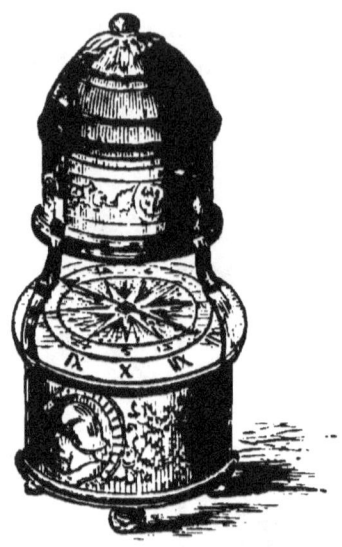

Ancient Table Watch, with Bell for striking (Temp. *circa* 1525).

A clock was purchased by Queen Victoria at
Strawberry Hill sale and is now at Windsor, which
was a present from Henry VIII. to Anne Boleyn,
and since from Lady Elizabeth Germains to Horace
Walpole.   It is described by Walpole as a clock of
silver gilt, richly chased, engraved and ornamented
with fleurs-de-lys, little heads, &c.   On the top sits a
lion holding the arms of England, which are also
on the sides.   On the weights are the initial letters of
Henry and Anne within true lover's knots, at the top
'Dieu et mon droit,' at the bottom 'the most happy.'

The emperor Charles V. (Henry's contemporary)

was so much pleased with observing the movements of time-pieces, that it is related of him, that he frequently sat after his dinner with a number of them upon the table before him, and that even after his retirement to the monastery of St Just he still continued his interest in them. He endeavoured to adjust their movements and keep them in order, but, upon finding it impossible to make any two watches agree with each other in keeping time, he was induced to reflect how much more absurd it must be for a man to attempt to regulate the more varied and hidden emotions of nations in consonance with those in his own breast. Ancient watches used to strike the time, and we read of Charles V. and Louis XI. that, watches having been stolen from them in certain crowds, the thief was detected by their striking the hour.

In 1577 Moestlin had a clock so constructed as to make just 2528 beats in an hour, 146 of which were counted during the sun's passage over a meridian, and thus determined its diameter. The alarum or alarm is one of the earliest additions to the mechanism of the clock, and is still used in Dutch clocks. This contrivance took its origin from the circumstance of prayers being read at stated periods in monasteries by night as well as by day, such an invention being of course of much service in arousing the priest to perform his duties.

In 1631 the Company of Clock-makers was

incorporated in England by Charles· I., who granted
them a charter prohibiting the importation of clocks,
watches, and alarms.   So that at this period Englishmen were sufficiently skilled in the production
of horological instruments to consider their importation in the light of an intrusion.   The Company consisted of a Master, three Wardens, and ten
or more Assistants who had power to make by-laws
for the government of all persons using the trade in
or within ten miles of London.   They were author-
ized to enter, with a constable or other officer, any
ships, vessels, warehouses, shops, or other places,
*where they shall suspect bad and deceitful works to be
made or kept,* and if such were found they seized them
in the King's name, and having proved their un-
worthiness, the objectionable works were broken up
and destroyed.   There are many instances mentioned
of such 'searches' upon the Books of the Company,
and although the practice has long become obsolete,
for in these times of free trade no such restrictions
would be tolerated, yet it would perhaps be found
that some testing by a modern 'searcher' or tester
would be of some protection to the public now-a-
days, when thousands of watches are sold which, like
Peter Pindar's razors, are intended rather for the market than for use.   The following are illustrations of
some timekeepers of the end of the sixteenth and the
beginning of the seventeenth century.

This is a very curious but not uncommon combination of the watch with the dial,—the latter being

Ancient Watch with Dial, 1580.

marked inside the watch-case and having a gnomon

moving on a hinge so as to allow of its lying flat and being enclosed within the case when not in use.

Our next illustration is of one of the earliest examples of a round watch made in England, the date being 1593. It contains not only a dial showing the hour, but a sort of general calendar in miniature.

English Round Watch, 1593.

Of much about the same date is the following example in silver and brass. It is of the same style of time-keeper, and shows how our forefathers liked to know not only the time of day but the period of the month; and how they watched the moon's changes,

and in a word made an almanac of their watches.
It was not an unusual thing for religious persons
who used rosaries at their devotions, to add to their

Oval Watch, 1593.

beads a miniature skull, with a view it may be to
remind themselves of the frailty of life by way of
stimulus to the preparation for the future state.
When watches were invented the Memento Mori
death's head was made into a watch-case, as in the
illustration on page 44.

The Lauder family, of Grange and Fountain Hall,
possess the *Memento Mori* Watch there engraved, they

having inherited it from their ancestors, the Setoun family. It was given by Queen Mary to Mary Setoun, of the house of Wintoun, one of the four Marys,

Ancient Ornamental Watch.

maids of honour to the Scottish Queen. This very curious relic must have been intended to be placed on a *prie-dieu*, or small altar, in a private oratory; for it is too heavy to have been carried in any way attached to the person. The watch is of the form of a skull : on the forehead is the figure of Death, standing between a palace and a cottage; around is this legend from Horace : ' *Pallida mors æquo pulsat pede pauperum tabernas Regumque turres.*' On the hind part of the skull is a figure of Time, with another legend from Horace: '*Tempus edax rerum tuque invidiosa vetustas.*' The upper part of the skull bears repre-

Old English Calendar Watch.

sentations of Adam and Eve in the garden of Eden, and of the Crucifixion, each with Latin legends; and between these scenes is open-work, to let out the sound when the watch strikes the hours upon a small silver bell, which fills the hollow of the skull, and receives the works within it when the watch is shut.

Nor about this time was the opportunity omitted of inculcating by means of pictorial watch illustrations,

' Memento Mori' Watch belonging to Mary Queen of Scots.

that Scriptural knowledge which was in the less educated times not so much taught by books as by pictures. The watch case given on the following page is of about 1600. It is obviously of English workmanship, and is a fair specimen of the period,—it may be, indeed, that, looking at it, one may well doubt whether art has much advanced in watch-ornamentation during the last 270 years or so.

We give our next illustration as another example of an ancient Table Watch. This watch has a revolving dial at the top, by means of which and the fixed point or hand the time is indicated (page 46).

Watch-case (*circa* 1600).

Such was the state of clockwork when Galileo, the great astronomer, then a medical student at Pisa, happened to discover, while gazing up at the roof of the cathedral when he should, perhaps, have been devotionally occupied, that the lamps suspended therefrom

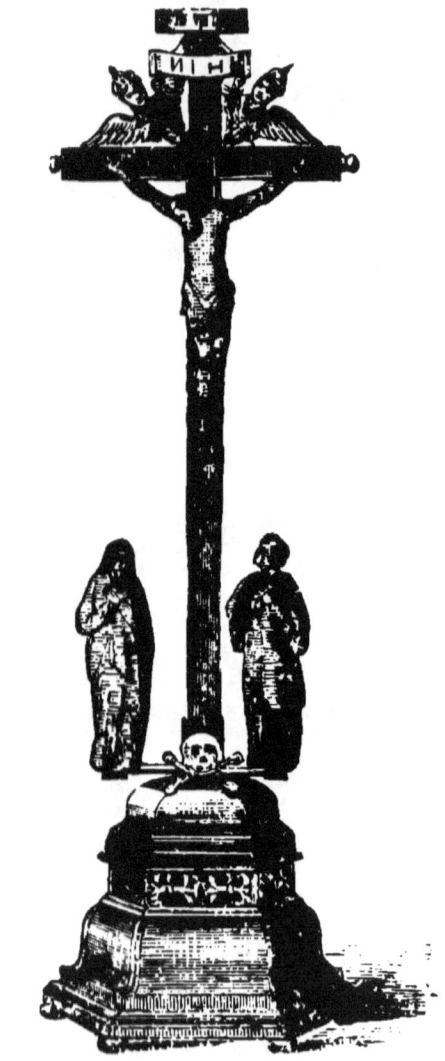

Table-Watch, *circa* 1630.

by chains of equal lengths, swung, and made their

vibrations in long or short arcs, in almost the same space of time,—a fact, the truth of which he ascertained by the beats of his pulse.

This isochronal property, as it was called, was described in a treatise which he published at Paris in 1639, entitled 'L'Usage du Cadron ou de l'Horloge physique universelle.' The first application which Galileo made of his discovery was the professional one of testing the rate and variations of the pulse, and it is even denied that he did more than suggest its applicability to clockwork.

The honours of the invention of the pendulum-clock have been contested by Vincentio Galilei, son of the great astronomer, who is said to have made a pendulum-clock at Venice in 1649, and Christian Huygens, a noted Dutch mathematician, who (in his excellent treatise, 'De Horologio Oscillatorio,' which was the foundation of most of the subsequent improvements in horometrical machines) clearly shows that he had constructed a pendulum-clock previous to 1658. His reputation will be somewhat obscured, however, if we yield to the claims of an Englishman named Richard Harris, an ordinary workman, who, it is said, invented the pendulum-clock which was fixed in the turret of St Paul's, Covent Garden, in 1642, and which is generally believed to have been the first pendulum-clock in Europe. The pendulum when first applied to clocks was suspended by a silken

cord, and the arc described by the bob or weight at
its end was a segment of a circle, but it being found
that this was in opposition to scientific knowledge,
and that the curve described by it should properly be
part of a cycloid or oval; Huygens tried to remedy
the error by causing the silk cord in its motion to
side or strike against a curved piece of brass, but he
thereby caused a greater error than he corrected.
Dr Hooke afterwards suspended the pendulum by a
thin flexible piece of steel, the bending of which, as
the pendulum swings from side to side, produces the
required cycloidal motion.   In 1658 Dr Hooke invented the Anchor Escapement which is still in use
together with the flexible spring to the pendulum

Ancient Silver Dial and Gold-cased Watch.   One hand.

above described.   Before, however, we proceed further
with our historical summary of the progress of watch

and clock making, it may be well to introduce here two illustrations of the watches worn by two of the most eminent Englishmen of about this period.

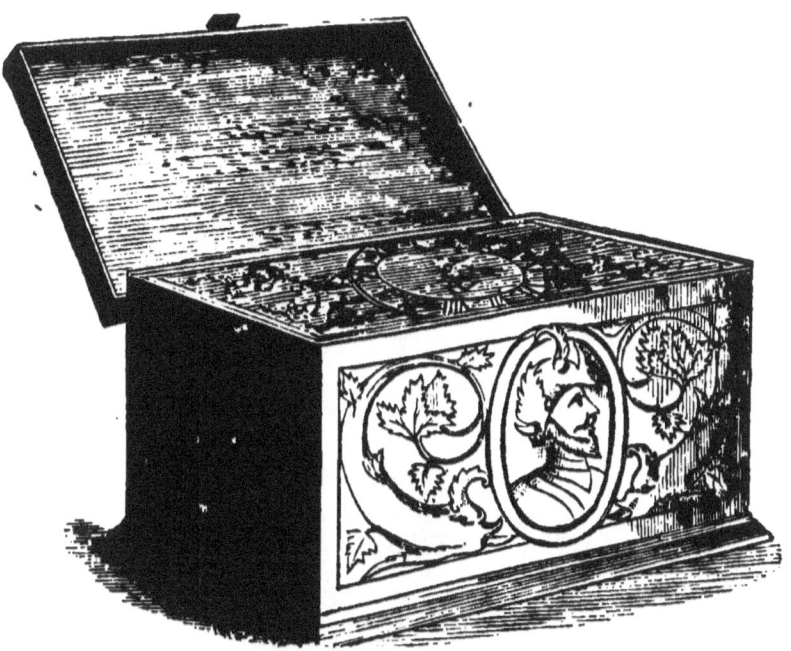

Ancient Box Watch.

The following watch was made about 1625 by Jonn Midwall in Fleet Street, who was Warden of the Clock-makers' Co. in 1635, and died about 1638. It is one of the early examples of a fob-watch. The case is of plain silver, fitted with glass over the face, and the chain of the same metal. The family crest of Crom-well was a demi-lion holding a ring in its paw, but the Protector substituted for the ring the handle of a

4

tilting spear, as engraved on the chain; the Cromwell
arms on the reverse, and the initials O. C., certify to

The Watch of Oliver Cromwell.

its genuineness. The arms as engraved and the
crest are identical with those on the banner used at

the Protector's funeral. The silver seals which were at one time attached to this chain are now absent, but they were a few years back in the possession of some descendants of the Cromwellian family, who allowed Sir Charles Fellows to take impressions of them. The watch, as it is here engraved, remained for upwards of a century in Holland, was there purchased by an English nobleman who presented it to his godson, and by him given to Sir C. Fellows, who believed that it was probably worn by Cromwell from 1625 until his death in 1658. In shape it reminds one of the Nuremberg egg watch. The following is an excellent example of

Early Ornamental Round Watch-case.

an early watch-case of the round shape still in use.

John Milton's Watch, made by William Bunting, London, 1631.

The history of this watch is somewhat singular.
From inscriptions which appear upon it, it seems to
have been made by William Bunting, (whose name
is entered upon the books of the Clockmakers' Co. as
elected to their court in 1645, he being then resident
in Pope's Head Alley, Cornhill,) in 1631, and presented to John Milton in the same year, which was
the date of the poet's leaving Christ's College, Cambridge, and taking up his residence with his father in
Horton, Buckinghamshire, he being then about 23
years of age.   From that time down to the early part

of the present century we have no record of the watch
or its possessors, but that in 1819 it was bequeathed
by the last surviving member of an old family in
Baltimore in the United States, who had treasured it
for some generations, to some old ladies residing near
London, the bequest including also a number of coins
of the reigns of Charles the 1st and 2nd, some medals
of Fairfax and others, as well as a few rings, but nothing of a later date. The chest which contained all
these relics safely arrived in London, and not long
after was, with its contents, offered for sale to an eminent chronometer-maker. The coins and medals being
in an excellent state of preservation were soon disposed
of at high prices, but the watch being only silver gilt,
and steel-faced, was considered to be of little value, and
a few shillings only were allowed as a fair price for it.
It was put into a drawer in its discoloured state and
there remained until 1828, when for the first time
the inscription on the face of it was discovered upon
its being accidentally cleaned up, and it was then presented to Sir Charles Fellows, well known for his
connoisseurship in such matters, and as a collector
of ancient timepieces. The maker's name upon the
inside of this watch is thus given : ' Gulielmus Bunting, London, 1631.' Sir Charles Fellows died in 1860
and bequeathed this one watch only to the nation ;
but his relict, Lady Fellows, who died in 1874, left the
whole of the celebrated collection of ancient watches

which her husband had brought together, to the British Museum.

In 1675 Tompion, under Hooke's direction, made a watch with a spiral balance for Charles II. Up to this period watches had but one hand and only pointed the hours, but the spiral pendulum spring having been applied to the balance, it regulated the oscillations with some nicety, and the minute wheel and hand were soon after added.

A watch was found upon Guido Fawkes when he was arrested for the Gunpowder Plot, which had been purchased by Percy and himself the day before 'to try conclusions' for the long and short burning of the touchwood with which he had prepared to set fire to the train of powder.

The following is one of the earliest examples we have met with of an

Early Watch, with double case.

It is apparently of French make, date of 1660, and is a remarkably neat and small specimen of the watches of that time.

The annexed illustration is a curious example of a watch of the date of 1580, to which a pendulum was added in 1670, and which is still capable of keeping time.

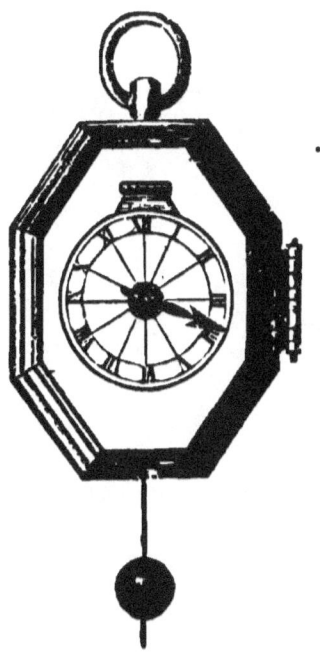

Ancient Watch with Pendulum.

Our next illustration is another specimen of antique design and ornamentation.

In 1676 Barlow, a London clockmaker, invented some mechanism whereby a person at night might ascertain, in the dark, the hour last struck, by pulling a certain part of it, and this contrivance gave the name of *repeater* to all timepieces in which it was used. For this invention Barlow tried to obtain a patent, but he

Ancient Brass Watch-case with lid protecting Dial.

was opposed by Daniel Quare and the Clockmakers' Company, who said that Quare was the original inventor. The question was tried by James II., and the decision given in favour of Quare. The following memorandum was entered upon the books of the Company with reference thereto. ' 1688, Sep. 29.—Be it remembered that in pursuance of the order of the Court of the 8th day of February, 1687-8, and according to the order of the Court of the 5th March, 1687-8, the patent endeavoured to be obtained by one Mr Edward Barlow, a priest, and to be granted to him by the king's majesty for his sole making and managing of all pulling repeating pocket-clocks and watches, he pretending to be the true and first inventor of that art and invention, was by diligence and endeavour of the Master, Wardens, and Assistants of this Company, with great charge and expense, which was borne by and out of the stock of the Company, very successfully prevented, and upon the the 2nd March, 1687-8, ordered by the king in Council not to be granted.'

In 1695 Tompion invented the cylinder escapement with horizontal wheel, but this was not brought into general use until some time after, when it was much modified. It was, however, a very valuable invention, and exercised considerable influence upon the shape of subsequent watches, inasmuch as it dispensed with the vertical crown wheel, and permitted them to be made more flat and therefore more conveniently portable.

We now come to the time when the use of jewels was first invented and applied; and as these, by being so hard and uninfluenced by friction as to allow the pivots to play without wearing away,—as metal would do by constant action,—afterwards gained for the English peculiar fame as manufacturers of watches,

we shall be excused for enlarging upon this point.
About the year 1700 Nicolas Facio, a native of
Geneva, having invented the use of jewels in watches,
and failed in his attempt to persuade the Parisian
watchmakers into the adoption of his notions, came
to London.   In May, 1705, he and two other watchmakers, Peter Debaufree and Jacob Debaufree, obtained a patent for his invention to extend over fourteen years.   In December, 1705, he petitioned, as we
shall presently see, to be granted a more extended
term, and then the Clockmakers' Company opposed
the application upon the ground of the invention not
being a novel one, and in proof of their statement
produced the watch, of which we give an illustration,
as made by Ignatius Huggeford, a member of their
own Company, some time before the application of the
pendulum-spring.   As this watch had a large amethyst mounted upon the cock or pivot of the balance-
wheel, the Committee of the House of Commons
were induced to decide against Facio's petition and
to throw out his Bill.

     This watch has since then obtained an extensive
historical reputation, and it is preserved in the archives
of the Clockmakers' Company as one of their most
valuable treasures, for it is the earliest known English
jewelled watch, and is the identical instrument produced before the House of Commons Committee, as
evidence to upset, and which did upset, poor Facio's

Ignatius Huggeford's Original Jewelled Watch.

claim for an extension of patent. Alas, for ancient
reputations, it has been but recently discovered that
Huggeford's watch was but a fraud, and that the
jewel on the cock which deceived the Parliamentary
Committee into supposing that Ignatius Huggeford,
an Englishman, had applied jewels to watches long
before Facio had been heard of, *has nothing to do with
the working* of the watch.   The jewel has been merely
stuck on, just in the place where a jewel should be;

but as it is only fixed to the surface of the brass and
no pivot plays in the jewel, it may be averred that
the amethyst has no more to do with the movement
of the watch than the silver ornaments on the watch-
case. It is clear by the words in Facio's petition that
his application of jewelling to watches was not merely
done with the idea of ornamenting them,—in that
there would have been no novelty,—and it seems
probable that the amethyst would have been placed
upon the face of the watch if the object of inserting
it anywhere had simply been ornamentation; to speak
plainly, none other than a fraudulent purpose could be
served by its being placed where it is. It is, we fear,
not impossible that the jewel was placed there at the
instance of some of the members of the Clockmakers'
Company, who, being perhaps jealous of the foreign
invention, and fearful of its effects upon their own private trade, were still unable to prevent the grant of a
patent, in May, 1703, for fourteen years to the inventor.
But by December of that year, when application was
made for the extension of the patent, they had had
time to consider affairs and to prepare their opposition.
We may believe this watch to have been Ignatius Huggeford's, and to have been all that it was sworn to be
by the members of that Company, but, when we
remark that neither is any mention whatever made
by them, nor, as far as it appears, any question asked
of them before the Parliamentary Committee as to the

jewel being upon the cock during the whole of the
time of its being in their possession, we cannot but
arrive at the conclusion that the jewel was placed
upon Huggeford's old watch—the date of which could
be shown—at the order of some of the members of the
Clockmakers' Company with the purpose of defeat-
ing the patent, and that the Committee of the House
of Commons were not as careful as they ought to
have been in inspecting the jewel, for if they had, they
must have seen the want of connexion between the
amethyst and the pivot, which, it was pretended, was
working in it. The probability is that at this time
our English watchmakers scarcely knew how to apply
a jewel, or otherwise they would have inserted the
pivot in a proper manner. The story is anyhow a
very extraordinary one, for, supposing the Clock-
makers' Company to be innocent of conspiracy on
the subject, it must have been a miraculously curious
whim which possessed old Huggeford to insert a jewel
as an ornament in a place where it would not be seen,
and still more wonderful that it should, sham as it
was, be placed exactly where it should suit the purpose
of after-litigation. Of course there can be no imputa-
tion arising out of this incident to affect the members
of the Clockmakers' Company of the present time,
for they are no more answerable for what was done
above a century and a half ago than the Parliament
of to-day is to be blamed for allowing the execution

of Charles I., or for enacting the laws which led to
the loss of our American colonies.

After the invention of jewels for watches came a
still more important discovery.

Since 1530, when Gemma Frisius first proposed to
ascertain the relative longitude of any place or ship at
sea, by means of an horological machine for indicating the time of the first meridian, the subject had
excited the attention of most of our philosophers, but
unavailingly, as there was then no chronometrical instrument, upon which reliance might safely be placed.
Huygens, in 1664, had contrived a timepiece actuated
by a spring and regulated by a pendulum, but the
pendulum was affected by the tossing of the ship, and
by a change of temperature, as well as being subject,
as was afterwards discovered, to a variation in weight
depending on the parallel of latitude. The Academy
of Sciences at Paris proposed, in 1720, a reward for
the best paper in reply to the question :—' What is
the most perfect method of preserving on the sea the
equable motion of a pendulum ?' The reward was
given to a Dutchman named Massy, but his plan was
not carried out. An English watchmaker named
Henry Sully happened to be about this time in Paris
directing a large manufactory of chronometers, and
he presented the French Academy with a marine
time-keeper of superior construction to the timepieces
of that period, and accompanied his gift by a memoir

describing it. Whilst still engaged in the study of his
art, Sully, who was a clever man, unfortunately died,
and the opportunity of advance seemed to have
passed away.

About this time Graham invented the Mercurial
Compensation pendulum, which consisted of a glass
or iron jar filled with quicksilver and fixed to the end
of the pendulum rod, which, when heat lengthened
the rod, expanded simultaneously the quicksilver, and
made the centre of oscillation to continue at the same
distance from the point of suspension. He afterwards
conceived a notion, which John Harrison subsequently
worked out, of making a compensation pendulum (or
a pendulum that should in itself contain the power of
equalizing its own action, whatever the change of temperature), forming it of various metals. In 1726 Harrison invented what is called the gridiron pendulum,
composed of nine rods, five of steel and four of brass,
which are so arranged that those which expand most
are counteracted upon by those of less expansion.
These two compensation pendulums, the gridiron and
mercurial, are still in use, and with slight improvements are found to keep to time very accurately.

The period had now arrived for the making
of marine time-keepers sufficiently accurate for
nautical use, and styled chronometers because they
are most accurate time-measurers. Their value to
navigators, and the immense impetus which would

by such instruments be given to the science of
navigation, had long been foreseen, but there were
many great difficulties in the way of obtaining
a perfect chronometer. The sailor, before the invention of this instrument, could ascertain the latitude of his ship at sea, by observation of the fixed
stars. Supposing these stars to have first appeared to
him in the zenith, and at his next observation to be
one, two, or three degrees south of the zenith, he
would know that he had sailed just so many degrees
north of the place in which he first observed them.
It was not, however, so easy for him to compute
longitudes, because the diurnal revolution of the earth
causes each meridian to pass successively under the
same stars. It was necessary to have an accurate
time-keeper, and to set it carefully to the solar time
of some port in the kingdom, whose longitude was
well known. The timepiece might then be carried
out in a vessel sailing abroad, and the computations
made by means of it would prove most wonderfully
exact and important. By simply observing the
moment at which the sun reached his meridian, when
of course it would be 12 o'clock at noon, solar time,
and then noting the difference between the solar time
thus ascertained and the time of the chronometer, the
mariner would be able by calculating 15 degrees to one
hour of time, or 15 geographical miles to one minute,
to make out his longitude. For example, if the time-

piece had been set to time at the meridian of Greenwich observatory, and if it be one o'clock by the
time-piece when it is mid-day, or meridian by the
sun, then the place in which the longitude is taken
must be in long. 15 degrees east of the meridian of
Greenwich, and if it be eleven o'clock by the chronometer when the sun attains his meridian, then the
place must be in long. 15 degrees west of the meridian
of Greenwich. It is not indispensably necessary,
that every chronometer used for maritime purposes
should keep time exactly with that of the Greenwich
observatory, or of any other instrument of known
excellence, provided always that its *rate* as seamen
call it, or the daily loss or gain of the chronometer, is
well ascertained, and so may be computed in the
calculations to be made. The indispensable requisite
of a chronometer, however, is that the daily loss or
gain shall not vary materially from itself at different
periods, or under the changes of temperature of different climates, and these qualities being found in
an instrument of any shape or make, constitute a
marine chronometer.

It will be generally obvious of what immense and
universal importance it was for men who 'go down
to the sea in ships and do their business on the great
waters' to be provided with a chronometer, and so be
enabled to calculate with a great degree of nicety,—
almost as a traveller by land learns his distances by

milestones and finger-posts,—the precise position
on the wide ocean of the vessel they are engaged
in navigating. So impressed was the British Parliament with the value of such an invention, that
as early as 1714, in the reign of Queen Anne, a
reward of £10,000 was offered, for any method for
determining the longitude within the accuracy of
one degree; of £15,000 within the limit of 40
geographical miles; and of £20,000 within the
limit of 30 geographical miles, or half a degree, provided such method should extend 80 miles from the
coast.   In 1736 John Harrison invented the first
chronometer, for which, after having added many
improvements, he received the gold medal of the
Royal Society in 1749. He still continued to per-
severe in improvements in his instrument, and at
last applied to be allowed to test its powers in such a
voyage as might permit of proof of its value. After
some time his application was granted, and his son,
William Harrison, embarked at Portsmouth, Nov. 18,
1761, for Jamaica. After eighteen days sailing the
vessel was computed to be 13° 50′ west of Portsmouth,
when the distance calculated by the watch was 15° 19′.
When the vessel arrived at Madeira, on the 9th of
December, it was found that the reckoning was corrected by the time of the piece, about a degree and a
half.   From Madeira to Jamaica the reckoning was
amended 3°; and at the several islands where the

ship touched the known longitudes agreed very
closely with those indicated by the chronometer.
Upon having returned again to England after a very
stormy voyage, the instrument underwent examination,
and its entire error amounted to $1^{m.}$ $53^{s.}$ 5. Harrison,
on this report being made, obtained from Parliament
a reward of £5000. A second experiment was
afterwards made in 1764, in March of which year
Harrison left Portsmouth with his instrument on
board the Tartar for Barbadoes. He had previously
conveyed to the Lords of the Admiralty his statement of the rates at which his chronometer went, and
the extent to which it was affected by change of
temperature. On May 13th the vessel arrived at
Barbadoes, and it was found that the amount of the
daily deviations from mean time was only $43^{s.}$ in ex-
cess. He returned to England after an entire voyage
of 156 days, and found that, allowing the gain of one
second per day as stated by him in his sealed ' rate,'
the whole gain was only 54^{s}. Harrison then was
examined by a committee appointed for the purpose,
and, having explained satisfactorily to them the principles of his instrument, he received another £5000.
A trial was then made by another person with a
chronometer made upon Harrison's plan, and this experiment also terminating favourably, the remaining
parliamentary reward was paid over to Harrison,
amounting in all to £20,000, a sum which was

still further increased by gratuities from the Board
of Longitude and the East India Company.

Harrison's improvements in time-measuring were
of considerable importance, as any one may readily
conceive, but he was sufficiently candid to acknow-
ledge that the balance, balance-spring, and compensation curb, as then used, were not simultaneously
affected by changes of temperature, that small pieces
were more readily affected than large ones, and pieces
in motion sooner than pieces at rest, whence he
concluded that if the provision for heat and cold
could properly be arranged in the balance itself, as in
his gridiron pendulum-clocks, the time might be
better kept.

Harrison's suggestion of a compensation balance
in lieu of a compensating curb, incited Peter le Roy,
a native of France, to the consideration of the question, and ultimately to the invention of a balance
acted upon by mercury and alcohol. The compensation was effected by the balance itself, which, carrying
the two thermometers, adjusted the mercury nearer or
farther from the centre of the balance, according to
the state of the atmosphere.

About this period there was considerable emula-
tion exhibited, both here and on the continent, upon
the subject of time-measuring. Sully had aided largely
in the advancement of the art of watchmaking in
London and Paris. Berthoud, Julien, and Pierre le

Roy made many ingenious propositions, and amongst others the invention of the detached escapement is attributed to the last-named.

In England we find the names of Arnold, Earnshaw, and Mudge associated about this date with the greatest improvements in chronometry, and as being those to whom prizes were at different times awarded by the Board of Longitude. In fact, few great inventions have since been made in the art, and our present high position as chronometer-makers is mainly due to the skill, energy, and perseverance then exhibited.

It would be superfluous to give any detailed description of the many valuable advantages derived from the science of horology, to which indeed all arts, sciences, trades, and callings are considerably indebted, and will probably be still more so in proportion to the increase of the use of steam-power and electricity. As by means of these recently-discovered powers mankind are enabled to compress into a day what would previously have required weeks and even months to accomplish, so must they regard with higher esteem, as these improvements are extended, the science by means of which they may divide and subdivide the precious minutes which are sufficient to perform so much. It will be worth while by way of illustration to point to the assistance given by horology to astronomical and nautical science. It is by

means of carefully-made and exact chronometers that
we calculate the distance and relations of the various
heavenly bodies to ourselves and to one another.
Having ascertained, by comparison, the rapidity of
light and sound, and that the former travels at the
rate of 192,000 miles per second, we discover that the
light of the sun requires eight minutes to reach the
earth, and thus compute the sun's actual distance from
us. So also observing the number of seconds which
elapse between the flash of lightning and the roll of
thunder, or between the flash and report of a cannon,
and remembering that in mild weather sound travels
at the rate of 1123 feet, and in frosty weather 1080
feet in a second, we shall be able, on making allow-
ances for the state of the atmosphere, to arrive at a
tolerably correct conclusion as to distances. It is by
means of a chronometer, though it be but a sand-
glass, that the sailor uses his log-line at sea and finds
the rate of his vessel's speed. His lead, enclosed in
the log, or wood, is attached to the log-line, which
has certain lengths called knots marked upon it for
nautical miles, and according to the knots paid out
in the half-minute of the sand-glass, so is the ship's
rate of sailing, i. e., if ten knots are passed in half a
minute the vessel's speed is at the rate of ten miles
an hour.

It would be both impossible and unnecessary to
describe the various experiments in which it is of

great consequence to measure time into minute proportions,—the number of these increases with advancing science; it will suffice if we have made the
subject sufficiently interesting to the general reader to
induce him to inquire further into the details.   It
is only by such investigations that he will be enabled
to give anything like a proper answer to the question
'What is Time?'

MODERN WATCHES:

THEIR VARIETIES AND MODES OF MANUFACTURE.

---

*'He that would wear a watch two things must do,—
Pocket his watch and watch his pocket too.'—Old Maxim.*

THE first possession of a watch by young persons
of either sex is perhaps one of the most vividly
retained of all their early memories. The sense of
responsibility, of importance, which such a wonderful
little piece of mechanism gives to them, the alacrity
with which they thenceforth note the flight of time
and compare the working of all other time-pieces, is
remarkable. One of the first things usually done by
the juvenile with his or her watch is, curiously enough,
to challenge thereby the performance of the old-
established time-pieces in the house,—even the infal-
lible old Hall Clock, a very Nestor among clocks,
does not escape scrutiny. Woe be to his ancient
reputation if, when 'weighed by the new balances'—
compensation or otherwise,—he be 'found wanting.'
The yet unfledged urchin will, upon the evidence of
his own newly-acquired chronometer, unhesitatingly

expose and denounce the slightest delinquency of the
antique time-piece, and pride and plume himself accordingly. At this time of day, when watches of a
sound and durable kind may be had for a comparatively small sum, and when education commences so
early, it may be supposed that youths attain earlier
to years of discretion, and so rise to the dignity of
watch-wearers sooner than their predecessors did.
Anyhow, the value of time can scarcely be incul-
cated at too juvenile an age, nor can it be brought
home to the mind of the pupil without providing
him with the means of studying the operations of his
own personal time-keeper. From the hour when
such a gift comes into his possession until the latest
day of his life a watch remains his indispensable
mentor, and, literally, his bosom-friend. There are
few, perhaps none, who can look upon the face of an
old watch, their day and night companion for many
years, without associating it with the bygone times
when it reckoned off for them their moments of pain
or anxiety, their joys and sorrows. There is perhaps
scarcely any memento of a friend or relative so sug-
gestive as that semi-living object which has been his
constant friend for so long, the chief valuable of all
his ' portable property.'

Our Old English popular rhymes and songs have
frequently been pointed with witticisms directed at
the care with which watches have been guarded, or

the dexterity with which they have been filched away.
Who can overlook the evergreen old dramatic joke,
of which the point consisted in connecting the time-
teller with the name of the ancient street-guardian;
e. g. :—

> 'I knocked him down, then snatched it from his fob.
> "Watch, watch!" cried he, when I had done the job;
> "My watch is gone!" said he: said I, "Just so,
> Stop where you are, watches were made to go."'

The Horizontal Watch.   The Skeleton Lever Watch.

Who can forget Dickens's description of the watch
of the wonderful Captain Cuttle, which, if you set so
far forward at night and so far backward in the
morning, was asserted to be 'a watch that would do

anybody credit;' or again, how can we omit mention
of that earlier Dickensian figure, mentioned by Sam

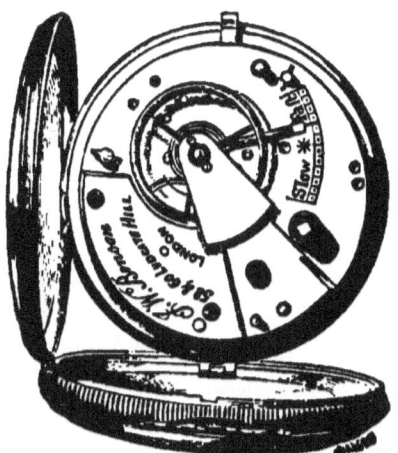

The Full Plate Patent English Lever.

Three-Quarter Plate English Lever.

Weller, wearing his enormous watch with so much
happy fearlessness, his seals dangling from his fob, the

continual temptation and despair of eager pick-pockets, whose ineffectual efforts to abstract the watch from such a tightly-protuberant stomach, were the never-ceasing delight of its jolly proprietor? Who shall narrate the characteristics of the various fashions in watches, and the trinkets that were worn along with them, the manners of the fine gentlemen who carried two at a time soon after swords were exchanged for walking-canes, and when pantaloons anticipated the easier but less graceful trowsers? Snuff-boxes, bag-wigs, pig-tails, high cravats, shoe-buckles, have all gone more or less out of fashion, but the watch is a peren-nial, which may indeed change its outer-casing and its decorations, like man himself, but knows no period of absolute disuse since first it started into being.

From the time when the first Nuremberg egg-watch was produced, there has always been noticeable an endeavour to make pocket time-pieces more and more small and portable so far as they could be made so consistently with their durability. Sometimes the love of very minute workmanship has been carried to an extreme, but toy-watches of eccentric shapes and patterns are but the few exceptions to the general rule, which has settled that usefulness and convenience are best provided for within certain moderate sizes, and that of all shapes the round and flat are the most easily carried. The great object of the watchmaker's ambition is to produce a time-keeper minutely accurate, and yet not so delicately constructed that it cannot withstand the rough usage to which even moderately careful wearers subject it.

It has been estimated that the manufacture of and trade in watches annually in England, France, Switzerland, and America, amount to over £5,000,000 per ann.; and that in Switzerland alone there are 38,000 persons, one-third of whom are women, engaged in the manufacture. It is probable that even the immense number of new watches thus annually produced barely exceeds the growing requirements of the people, who, as they increase in intelligence and receive higher wages, soon learn the advantage of personally possessing a pocket time-keeper, and make it accordingly their first ambition to purchase one. The Watch Clubs which are formed in the various towns and rural districts throughout the kingdom enable this desire to be gratified at but small pecuniary inconvenience, inasmuch as payment is thus made in small instalments at fixed intervals, and the watch is bought with sums which might have been spent thoughtlessly and to no permanent benefit. This first lesson in thrift having been well learnt, and the result being so palpably beneficial to those who exercise it, has often laid the basis of a regular habit of economy.

The motive power in the watch is derived, not as in the clock from weights, but from a spiral spring

called THE MAINSPRING, set in a drum or barrel, and
any inequality in the pressure of the spring is fatal to
regular time-keeping. A highly tempered and finished
spring is a primary requisite in watch-making; in
order to provide for the uniform transmission of
motive power from the barrel throughout the train to
the escapement, the fusee and chain are used, the
fusee being a hollow-sided cone, and the chain round
it. When the spring is wound up its force is of
course greatest, for the chain is then acting on the
smallest end of the fusee. The proportions of the
barrel to the centre wheel, and the size of the teeth
in that wheel, have all to be carefully planned, and
adjusted to one another, and these all again to the
moving of the hands upon the dial.

The ESCAPEMENT is one of the most important
parts of the mechanism of a watch. It may be one
of either of the following.

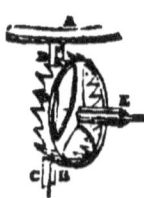

Verge
Escapement.

The *Verge* escapement, as applied
to Watches, will be seen annexed. A,
part of the balance; *b*, the verge body;
c, c, the pallets; D, the escape-wheel;
E, escape-wheel pinion. The verge or
arbor B of the balance has two pallets,
c, c, which stand out at right angles, so as to be acted
on alternately by the sloping teeth in the opposite
sides of the crown or escapement-wheel, c.

The *Horizontal* escapement, on the following page,

so called because of the escape-wheel acting horizon-
tally to the axis of the balance.   This invention was
perfected by Graham, after the death of the inventor,
his master and friend, Thomas Tompion.   a, the·
escape-wheel, hav-
ing pins or stems
rising from it, on
the tops of which
are teeth of a wedge-
like form, of such a

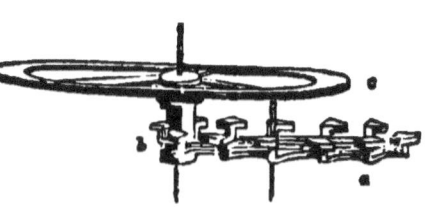

Horizontal Escapement.

length as to permit little freedom within and without
the cylinder b, which is firmly fixed to the balance c.
Although b is one piece, the two edges of the hollow
part serve as distinct vallets, inasmuch as they receive
alternately, during each vibration of the balance, an
impulse from the curved outer edge of each tooth in
succession; and as the wedge-shaped tooth passes from
the pallet, the coming tooth falls on to the circular part
of the cylinder, and there remains until the return of
the balance, when that tooth which had previously
rested on the circular portion of the cylinder, comes
upon the edge or pallet, gives impulsion to the balance
c, and falls upon the concave portion of the cylinder,
and there remains until the balance again returns, when
another impulse takes place, and so on in succession.
Watches having the cylinder escapement were not
known in France till the year 1728, when Julien le
Roy obtained one of them from Graham.

The *Duplex* escapement is of a very peculiar construction, and nearly approaches the chronometer; it
is probable that it was originally invented by Dr Hooke,
although, as we now have it, it came from the hands
of Tyrer. It is seen in our illustration. A, the escape-
wheel; B, the escape-wheel teeth; c, the balance; D,
the pallet of impulse; E, the ruby roller; F, a notch
in ditto : 1, 2, 3, cogs or upright teeth on the rim of
the escape-wheel. The balance is supposed to be
turning downwards towards the right, the tooth of the
escape-wheel just resting against the ruby roller.
When this (which is called the return) vibration is
complete, the balance, by the strength of the hair

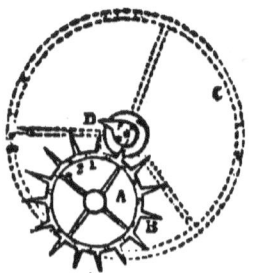

Duplex Escapement.

spring, is carried in the opposite
direction, and as the notch F
passes the tooth of the escape-
wheel, this latter is enabled to
pass the roller, and the upright
tooth or cog falls upon the pallet
D, and thus gives impulse to the
balance. The next straight tooth
of the escape-wheel is now resting against the roller c,
and the same operation again takes place. This
escapement is much superior to the horizontal, and is
almost independent of oil. It can carry a balance of
much greater weight, and when well made performs
admirably. Duplex watches, however, should never
be selected by persons who are accustomed to ride on

horseback, as these instruments are liable to be affected by any sudden motion. Even the stepping quickly from a vehicle mày stop them, and yet the escapement be as perfect as possible. They are only adapted for persons of very quiet habits. Thomas Mudge, in the year 1766, introduced an admirable invention, which, after many alterations and improvements, is now universally known as the '*Patent Detached Lever*' escapement, represented by—*a a* the escapement-wheel, *b b* the ruby pallets, *c* the lever, *d* the balance. On the axis of the balance *d*, towards the lever *c*, is a

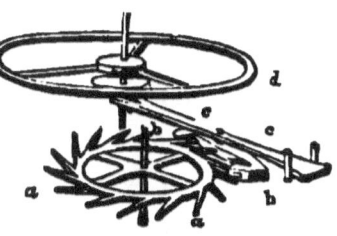

Lever Escapement.

small disc of steel, into which is inserted a small pin made of ruby. This pin fits with great nicety into a notch or opening in the end of the lever *c*, upon which are firmly fixed the two pallets *b b*, into which are secured rubies very finely polished. The balance in its vibration on either side, carrying with it the steel disc and ruby pin, causes that pin to enter the notch in the lever and carry the lever with it, and at the same time, to draw the pallet from the tooth of the escapement-wheel *a*. Power being exerted upon this wheel by the mainspring, the wheel tooth gets disengaged from the locking-face of the pallet, forces itself down the slopes of the pallet, and thus

6

gives impulse to the balance. At each vibration the
same unlocking takes place, but as soon as the wheel
tooth falls from the slope, the opposite pallet is prepared to receive the advancing tooth of the escapement-wheel, and so on in succession beat after beat
takes place. So excellent was this escapement considered a few years back, that chronometers were
made upon the principle, and placed in the Royal
Observatory for public trial. But since then many
improvements have been made in it, so that makers
are now enabled to produce a pocket watch, with the
short angle lever escapement, which marks time at a
steady rate of within four or five seconds weekly,—a
rate which approaches so near to the time-keeping of
a pocket chronometer, that unless the minutest exact-
ness for some specific purpose is required, the last-
named watch is all that can be wished for.

About the year 1780 was invented the escapement
which is now denominated the Detached or *Chronometer Escapement* (see opposite page), the principles of
which are the nearest approach to perfection, the impulse to the balance being given at the centre of vibration. A is the escape-wheel, B the escape-wheel teeth,
C the roller let on the verge, or axis of the balance.
This roller is a circle of polished steel, with a notch
cut out of it, into one side of which, D, a flat polished
piece of ruby is inserted for the acting part. Below
this steel roller, carried on the same verge, is a smaller

roller of steel (E), denominated the discharging pallet,
having a sapphire fixed on its
outer edge. F is a slender
spring, which is screwed at I
to the stouter one, having its fixture at the stud L,

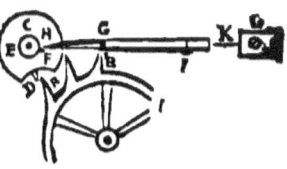

Chronometer Escapement.

and polished away very thin at K, in order that it may
bend readily, so as to cause very little resistance to
the balance while forcing it on one side. G is a projecting piece, carrying an upright pin made of ruby,
against which the wheel tooth B rests; at B is a
small screw against which the spring L K G strikes,
and thus prevents it from springing too far back.
The action of these parts is as follows :—When at
rest the circular edge of C is just clear of the two teeth
of the wheel B, which cannot be set in motion while
E and G remain quiescent; G rests against the screw
at B, and the tooth resting against the locking pallet
G, the escapement-wheel cannot turn. To set the
chronometer going it is necessary to give it a rotary
motion, which sets the balance in action. This
causes the lower piece on the verge (called the lifting
piece or discharging pallet) to strike against the end
of the spring F, which, from its over-lapping the curved
end of the prolonged spring K G, pushes it back, and
thus releases the pin or locking stone G from before
the tooth of the wheel : that is, it unlocks the escapement-wheel, which is immediately set in motion by

the force of the mainspring. The same vibration
given to balance and verge brings the ruby pallet D
round before the tooth B, which strikes against it and
carries it round. The recoil of the spring F has now
brought the locking pallet G to catch the tooth B, the
escapement-wheel is thus again stopped. But the
stroke of the tooth upon the face of the ruby pallet D
has driven the balance on in its vibration till it is
counteracted by the tension of the balance spring,
which brings it back again; in this return vibration
the lifting pallet E, by its curved back, pushes the
slender spring F before it, and passes it without affect-
ing K, G, which is stiff enough to remain unmoved by
F, even when this strikes and rests against it in recoil-
ing. The wheel, therefore, continues locked on the
upright pallet G, and the vibration proceeds uncon-
trolled till the great pallet is again brought round,
and the balance spring again checks the vibration, the
above process being repeated. In this escapement,
consequently, part of one vibration in one direction,
and the whole of that in the other, is performed without the balance being in any way under the influence
of the motive power; while the parts are so contrived
that the impulse given by the tooth of the escape-
wheel, affects in a very slight degree the natural
motion of the balance. It can be easily understood
that the lifting pallet E can pass the spring F in one
direction without moving K and G, while in the other
it carries E and G with it.

Several appliances have been from time to time introduced to correct the error in time-keeping caused by variations in the temperature, but none have come into such general use as that known by the term *Compensation Balance,'* invented by Thomas Earnshaw, of London, and for which he received a government reward. This balance, when properly adjusted, causes the watch to keep the same time whether the temperature be 32 deg. or 90 deg.; while without it a watch will show a considerable difference in time, on being merely transferred from the

Compensation Balance.

pocket to the dressing-table, where, probably, the temperature would not be so high.   Our woodcut represents a balance of this kind; the divided rim A A, is composed of steel and brass run together by fusion, the more expansible metal, brass, being placed outwards, the result of which is as follows: —Heat elongates the pendulum spring, and thereby causes a slower vibration of the balance.   The same amount of heat will also expand the metals composing the balance ; but as the inner rim of steel does not expand so freely as the outer one of brass, the conflicting action of the two tends to draw the free end of the circular rim inwards towards its centre, and thus decreases in all but one direction the diameter of the balance.   This decrease tends to *quicken* its vibration, and thus counteracts the effect of the elongation of the pendulum spring. In cold temperatures the pendulum spring is contracted, making the vibrations quicker, but the contraction of the brass rim draws the free end outwards, thus increasing its diameter, retarding its vibrations, and counteracting the effect of the contraction of the pendulum spring.

Many contrivances have been introduced to test the equality of compensation balances, but the majority have been abandoned from the circumstance that the heat was not equally distributed to the watches under trial. In pursuance of this object, an oven was invented, heated by hot water, which answers the desired end. It is an apparatus made of copper, two feet high, thirteen inches broad, and eight inches deep. From the top to the bottom, at the distance of fifteen inches, it is divided into two compartments. All around the upper one (except the front, which has a glass door through which the chronometers and watches are seen without opening it) is one inch of water. It has a chamber thirteen inches high, eleven inches broad, and seven inches deep for the reception of chronometers and watches. The water is introduced at the top in the same manner as a solar lamp is supplied with oil. The bottom compartment contains a jet of gas, which can at pleasure be regulated so as to keep the watch at any required temperature. The heat radiated from the inner surface of the chronometer chamber is thus equally distributed among the instruments under trial. A thermometer placed within the upper chamber indicates the temperature, and by this simple apparatus a watch can be regulated with the greatest nicety to suit the particular climate into which it may be taken.

The DIAL AND HANDS should be sufficiently in contrast one to the other to show the time at a glance. Dials are sometimes made of gold or silver, but these are not so distinctly seen as white enamelled dials, with black figures or numerals, and dark blue steel hands; the enamelled faces, although, perhaps, more brittle than gold or silver dials, are therefore in greatest request. Up to a comparatively recent date the seconds' hand was placed upon the level face of the watch, but sunk seconds are now everywhere in use, even in the cheaper sorts of watches. The chief objection taken to the sunk seconds is that it disfigures the dial by breaking the uniformity of the numeral letters, the VI being of course obliterated to make room for it, but this obliteration seems of smaller consequence than the confusion which may arise from the use of longer seconds' hands and their being at any time mistaken for that of the hour or minute.

The JEWELLING of a watch is an important part of its manufacture, inasmuch as it is by means of jewels that durability is chiefly secured. Watch pivots would rapidly wear out the metal in those parts in which there is continual friction, and jewelling has therefore become general. The watchmaker uses for his best watches a peculiarly hard kind of ruby, which has been known to withstand the wear and tear of the best part of a century without showing symptoms of yielding, whereas inferior jewels are perhaps scarcely so hard as the best tempered metal.

The FRAME, usually of brass gilt, sustains both ends of each axis, and is now principally designed to fit a full-plate movement or a three-quarter-plate movement. The former is undoubtedly the more simple construction, but with considerable disadvantage in taking to pieces the watch and putting it together again when repairs are needed. The examination of the escapement in a full-plate watch, and the cleaning, or altering, or oiling which may be needed, cannot be done without taking the whole movement to pieces. The three-quarter-plate movement is not only preferable on account of its superiority in respect to solidity, and the economy of labour in its manufacture, but from its being flatter than the full-plate watch, and allowing of repairs being more easily made.

The WATCH-CASE, which used to be of various materials, such as tortoiseshell, pinchbeck, or one of the precious metals, is now almost universally of gold or silver. Silver cases are invariably of the standard required by the law and stamped accordingly; gold cases vary in fineness,—some being made and stamped

of 9 carat gold, but the best for wear, and as such
preferred by the best makers, are of 18 carats, and are
stamped as such with the hall mark, usually in three or
four places,—on the bow, the pendant, and the inside
of the case.   Much depends upon the care with which
this part of a watch is finished, for an ill-fitting case
admits dust which renders frequent cleaning necessary,
and prevents accurate time-keeping.   After the case-
maker has constructed the case it has to pass through
several hands before it is completed,—for instance, it
is one man's work to fit the works to the case by
making the joint at the 12 o'clock and the bolt at
6 o'clock, and to supply the wheels to propel the
hands ; it is another's to perform the part of engine-
turner, and to mark the case with those curiously
intricate lines whose wonderful precision cannot be
secured by mere hand-work, but by a combination of
mechanical and human labour; another's to finish
the joints, or, as the uninitiate would perhaps call
them, the hinges ; and last of all the fitter of the case
with springs, and polisher to give the necessary finish.
In the same way has each part of the mechanism of
the interior passed through a series of workmen's hands.
Nearly every wheel and pinion has been separately
made by men whose entire time is given to the per-
fecting of their several branches of labour, the sub-
divisions of which and their ramifications would need
many lengthy chapters of description, to do them

justice. The escapement is of itself a distinct depart-
ment requiring a number of co-operating hands, from
those which first shape the metal to the balance-
maker working in brass, steel, or gold, and the final
adjustment of the escapement-maker. The chain,
the spring, the jewelling, the brass-work, the engraving, the gilding, have each their separate history, some
of them being brought from one district and some
from another, to be put together in the watch manufactory, which is finally to produce them unitedly as
an entire watch. Division of labour provides a larger
amount of skilled work, and a more satisfactory
result, than any other method. The workman whose
entire life is spent in making the head of a pin or in
fixing it on, will do his work better than the man,
however clever he may be, who should attempt to
make the whole pin; and not only is the work thus
better done, but it is done by combination much more
expeditiously and cheaply. All that the watch-
manufacturer can do by way of choosing his materials is, however, of course, but antecedent to his own
work of actual construction, of finishing, examining,
and regulating. He is to the watch what the architect is to a house; the latter is none the less the
rearer of the structure because he did not himselt
make the bricks, or saw the timber, or mix the mor-
tar. Each subordinate brings certain materials to the
hand of the constructor, and he combines them, and

gives them their places, he turns them into shape and produces them as a perfect whole. So the watch-manufacturer, instead of going himself back through the various stages of work which in Nuremberg-egg time had, perhaps, all to be done by one pair of hands, chooses, adapts, combines the labours of hundreds of busy collaborateurs, all of whom have made portions and pieces,—he alone makes the Watch.

COMPLICATED WATCHES are so called because besides the ordinary watch movement they possess other mechanism more or less complicated, by means of which they can indicate special portions of time,—as for instance the *Chronograph*, which marks on its dial the fifth of a second; the *Quarter*, and *Half-Quarter*, and *Minute Repeaters*, which furnish the time in the dark to within a minute, and are invaluable to invalids and blind persons; the *Clock-Watch*, which strikes the hours even in the pocket; the *Clock-Watch Repeater*, which strikes and repeats; the *Independent split Centre Seconds, and Fifth Seconds Watch*, which shows (by comparing the one with the other) the lapse of time to the fifth of a second; the *Perpetual Calendar Watch*, which shows the day of the week and of the month, the name of the month, the phases of the moon, &c.; the *Perpetual Calendar Repeating Watch*, which in addition to the calendar shows by a repeater the hour, quarter, and minute; and the *Meridian Watch*, which shows the time of day in any

given number of places in any part of the world. A
few words descriptive of the peculiarities of each of
the above complicated watches will be necessary here,
and observing the sequence as above, the following
brief particulars will perhaps be sufficient for ordinary
reference, or for being kept in memory.

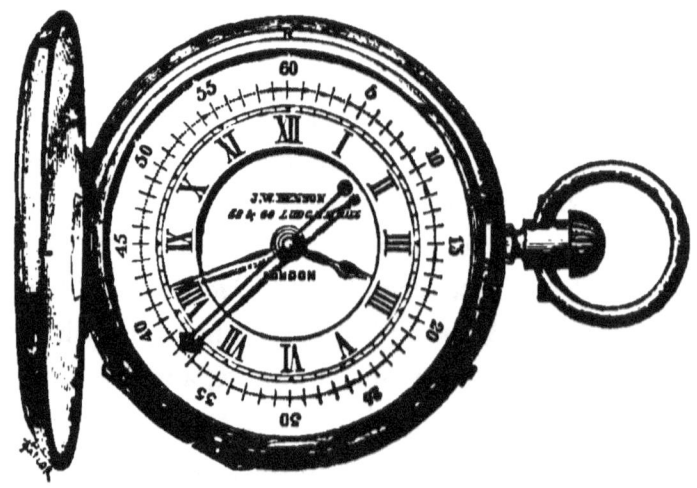

The CHRONOGRAPH is undoubtedly the most perfect instrument yet invented for marking the exact
time occupied by certain rapid movements or events
or performances,—and is therefore well adapted for
astronomical and medical observations, for timing
machinery, for indicating the speed of a race, and of
similar quick events even to the tenth of a second.
It consists of an ordinary quick train lever movement
on a scale sufficiently large to carry the hands for an

8-inch dial. The peculiar feature of the chronograph is its second hand, which is double, consisting of two distinct hands,—the one lying over the other. The lower of the two is furnished at the tip with a small reservoir having an extremely small orifice below; over this orifice the point of the upper hand is bent so as to fall exactly upon the puncture, and to convey through it, as with a pen, the ink held in the reservoir. The mode of operating with the chronograph at a race has been thus described. 'The chronograph is held firmly in the left hand of the operator, who watches the starters, but need not trouble himself to keep at the same time an eye upon the dial. At the moment of the start he presses the finger or thumb of his right hand gently upon the button of the pendant, and instantly a black dot is deposited on the dial, and—the operator being ready to touch the button at the precise moment of the finish, and thus to complete what we may call the chronogram of the event—the exact length of the race is registered, even to a decimal fraction of a second, and an indisputable record written by the instrument itself in black and white. The chronograph, it should be mentioned is, apart from its chronographic mechanism, an excellent time-keeper, and may be worn as an ordinary watch, being the same size as a gentleman's lever watch.

REPEATING WATCHES are now made so as to

require no key. They are constructed with a lever or chronometer escapement, and are known according to their method of repeating,—the ordinary *Repeater* strikes the hours and quarters,—the *Half-quarter Repeater* strikes the hours, quarters, and half-quarters,—the *Minute Repeater* strikes hours, quarters, and minutes. The first tells the time in the dark or to the blind person to within a quarter of an hour, the second tells it within seven minutes and a half, the third tells it to the minute.

The CLOCK WATCH and CLOCK REPEATING WATCH are also made so as to need no key. They strike the hours and quarters while being worn in the pocket, and have not only the two trains of wheels for going and striking as in a clock, but a third train provided for repeating purposes. Both mainsprings are wound up by the same winder by a forward and backward action of the pendant. They are constructed with either Lever, Duplex, or Chronometer Escapements, and some are provided with compensation balances adjusted to act equally at extremes of temperature.

THE INDEPENDENT CENTRE SECONDS WATCH is peculiarly adapted for the use of the medical profession. By means of its two trains it carries, besides the ordinary hands denoting hours, minutes, and seconds, a long seconds hand which can be stopped without stopping the watch. It is made with a stem winder, and therefore requires no key.

THE SPLIT CENTRE SECONDS is not quite so
complicated as the last named. It has two centre
second hands revolving round the dial, the one directly over the other, as also, in another part of the
dial, a small hand revolving five times in a second.
Upon pressing a stop-piece one of the long second hands
is stopped, and another pressure will stop the other
—the space between the two hands will then indicate
precisely the time occupied by the event which it is
desired to measure.   Another push to the stop-piece
will make both hands again fly together, and enable
the operator it may be to make a new experiment or
observation.

THE PERPETUAL CALENDAR KEYLESS WATCH,
shows on its dial the year, the month of the year,
the day of the month, the day of the week, the phases
of the moon, as well as hours, minutes, and seconds.
It requires no setting, as the old-fashioned Calendar
Watch did at certain intervals, but, by a very ingenious contrivance, the changes from month to month,
as for example from February 28th to the 1st of
March, or from 30th or 31st of other months to the
1st of the next, are all performed by the watch, which
also of itself marks the extra day for Leap Year.
When to all the above are added, as is sometimes
done, the Minute Repeating Work to repeat the hours,
quarters, and minutes, it may be said that the power
of complication can no farther go within the limits of

the small box which is called a watch case,—for these
watches are provided with either Lever, Duplex, or

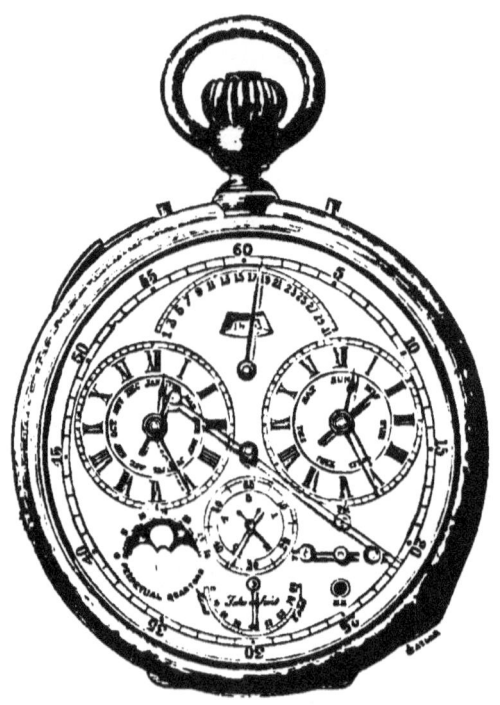

The Perpetual Calendar Keyless Watch.

Chronometer Escapements as may be preferred, and
with compensation balances adjusted to serve in extremes of temperature.   But in the examples set forth
in the following illustrations, it will be seen that
superadded to all the foregoing are a thermometer,
and an index showing the calendar by the old and
new style, as indicated by the words Gregorian and
Russian,—the former referring to Pope Gregory who

decreed the alteration to the new style, and the latter to the fact that the Russians still reckon by the old style.

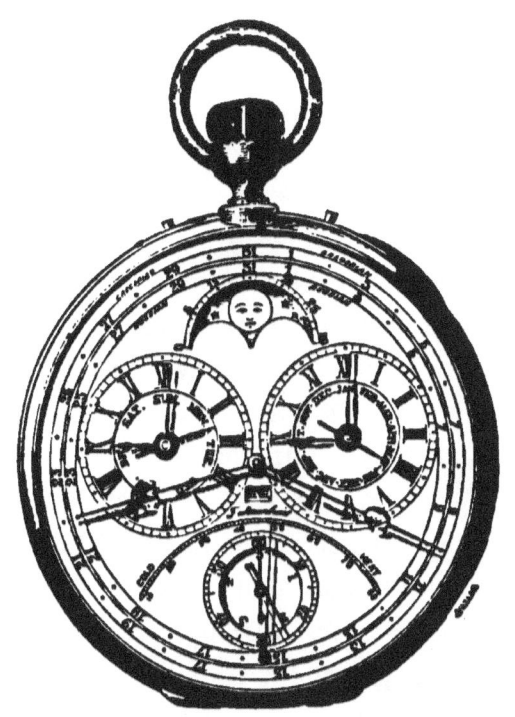

THE COMPLICATED PERPETUAL CALENDAR AND INDEPENDENT SECONDS KEYLESS WATCH, is another example of this kind of mechanism, which, without being re-set from time to time for leap year and other changes, keeps a perpetual register of seconds, minutes, hours, days, weeks, months, and years, shows Old and New Styles, the phases of the moon, and variations of heat and cold. It has

7

also two separate trains of wheels and two mainsprings, both of which are wound up by the button at the pendant.   It will be seen that the dial
has two hour circles with hour and minute hands
showing separate time.   Below the centre is the sunk
seconds dial with two seconds hands, the one over the
other, and each working independently, so that the
one may be stopped by a push at the button of the
pendant and yet the other go on, to be in its turn
stopped, so that the operator may use it as a stop-
watch.   Underneath the hour hands of each circle is
the hand showing the month and the day of the week.
The two centre hands, with the letters G and R, are
pointing to the days of the month, and showing the
Gregorian and Russian day.   In the small square
space just below the centre is the year, and below this
and lying over the second hands is another hand
pointing to the degrees of temperature to which the
watch is exposed; near the top of the dial is a small
plate showing the phases of the moon,—the position
indicated in this illustration is that of full moon.

The MERIDIAN WATCH shows the time of day in
any number of places in any part of the world.   It
is set to Greenwich time, and marks the difference
between this and the time of all the great metropo-
litan cities in both hemispheres,—as St Petersburg,
Constantinople, New York.

The name CHRONOMETER,—derived from the

Greek, and meaning a time-measurer,—is chiefly applied to marine time-pieces and to watches which

The Meridian Watch.

have been carefully made with chronometer or detached escapements and compensating balances serving to equalize the effects of heat and cold. MARINE CHRONOMETERS are the chief instruments for discovering the longitude at sea, and are therefore subjected to special tests at Greenwich observatory and elsewhere before being sent on board ship. They have dials of three or four inches in diameter, hour, minute, and second hands, besides a hand to indicate the day upon which the instrument was last wound up,—and they are made to go from two to eight days. Being well mounted on gimbals inside of an air and water-tight brass case they do not toss about with the

motion of the ship but always preserve their equilib-
rium. For extra protection they are generally kept
enclosed in a mahogany case. Chronometers have
for their motive power, like watches and spring-clocks,
a main-spring acting on the fusee by the chain,—as
the chain winds upon the fusee the force of the spring
is so equalized that it is exactly the same whatever the
position of the chain. When marine chronometers
are sent to the Greenwich observatory they are subjected, under the directions of the Astronomer Royal,
to extreme degrees of heat and cold, and up to the
year 1835 prizes were awarded to those makers whose
instruments best stood these tests; but such prizes are
no longer given. It has even been found that chronometers which are most capable of withstanding
extremes of temperature are not the most perfect in
medium climates, and this discovery brought about
new endeavours and a new suggestion known as the
Auxiliary or Secondary Compensation.

MARINE TIME-PIECES FOR SHIPS AND YACHTS.
These instruments possess the character rather of
clocks than of chronometers, inasmuch as they are
designed to hang against a bulk-head, and they
would not appear unsuitable to house purposes. They
are portable and useful clocks, and having a lever
escapement with compensated balance, the motion of
the vessel does not affect them. Some yacht time-
pieces are constructed so as to chime the quarters or

tunes, and to strike the ships' bells as well as the hours. They are also sometimes placed in very handsome cases of bronze or ormolu, decorated with special designs to illustrate the name of the ship or yacht to which they belong. Their movements are not as accurately adjusted as those of Marine Chronometers, but they, nevertheless, are made to keep time excellently.

KEYLESS WATCHES.

THE keyless mechanism to a watch is one of the great modern improvements in watch work; it does away with the old-fashioned key, with which so many persons have ruined their watches, the watch is wound by turning a knurled knob, placed on the handle or bow (see illustrations, pp. 96-7) instead of by the ordinary means : the hands are set in the same way, with the addition of pressing a small projection on the side of the case. The advantages of these improvements are obvious; the case, which never need be opened in winding, is made air tight and dust tight, thus preserving much longer the fluidity of the oil, and greatly prolonging the intervals between the necessary cleaning of the watch. Besides which, the keyless mechanism being attached to the watch, the key can never be lost or mislaid, or worn out.

*Strict attention to the following simple Directions is
necessary for the proper Management of a Watch.*

1st.—Wind your watch as nearly as possible at
the same time every day—the morning is the best.
Care should be taken to avoid sudden jerks.

2nd.—Be careful that your key is in good condi-
tion, free from dust and cracks. It should not be
kept in the waistcoat pocket, or in any place where it
is liable to rust or get filled with dust.

3rd.—Keep the watch while being *wound* steadily
in the hand, so as to avoid all circular motion.

4th.—The watch, when hung up, must have support, and be perfectly at rest; or, when laid horizon-
tally, let it be placed on a soft substance for more
general support, otherwise the action of the balance
will generate a pendulous motion of the watch, and
cause much variation in time.

5th.—The hands of a duplex or chronometer
watch should never be set backwards; in other
watches this is a matter of no consequence, but to
avoid accidents it is much better to set them always
forward.

6th.—Should the watch vary by heat or cold, as
when worn or not worn in the pocket, the hands may
be set to time, but the regulator should not be altered;
but when it is found necessary to alter the regulator,
it should be done gently, and very little at a time.

7th.—*The glass should never be opened in watches that are set and regulated at the back.*

8th.—Keep your watch-pocket free from dust or nap, which generally accumulates in the pocket when much used.

9th.—Be cautious to whom you give your watch ·for repair; the best watches being frequently irretrievably damaged by inexperienced workmen. Never allow your watch to go longer than two years without being cleaned. .

HOUSE CLOCKS.

BETWEEN the small wooden Dutch Clock of the value of but a few shillings, and the carefully-made Regulator Clock which costs ten times as many pounds, there is necessarily a wide difference; but both may be considered as within the general designation, 'House Clocks.' The former sometimes go for many years with a fair amount of regularity, and are found to be useful to the humblest classes, whose hours for early morning labour are frequently regulated thereby. The latter are made with such accuracy as to correct the time of other clocks, such as turret and church clocks, which are more exposed to the influence of the weather, and are necessarily made upon a coarser scale. In large mansions there is no handsomer or more necessary appointment for the hall or vestibule than a fine eight-day clock, 'to welcome the coming, speed the parting guest,' and to give the time of day to the entire household.

It would be worth while, did our purpose admit of it, to write a chapter on the longevity of Clocks, by

way of showing the comparative cheapness of the
solid, well-built piece of mechanism whose every item
has been carefully put together of the very best and
most durable materials by the most skilled horologers.
For generation after generation such a sound, well-
made time-piece shall keep accurate time, and put to
shame by both its performance and the insignificant
expense of keeping it in order, the instruments of, it
may be, more showy appearance, but less careful
construction.   Such a clock descends from father to
son until its own age is scarcely to be remembered,
and is regarded as one of the family heir-looms,—
nay, as more,—almost, we would say, as a friend
familiar with all the scenes and experiences which
have made up family history.   It was of such a clock
that Longfellow wrote—

'By day its voice is low and light,
But in the silent dead of night,
Distinct as a passing footstep's fall,
It echoes along the vacant hall,
Along the ceiling, along the floor,
And seems to say, at each chamber-door,
    For ever—never,
    Never, for ever.'

It was such an one that Dickens apostrophized in
that wonderfully-genial style which won for him so
much love and fame :—' My old cheerful, companion-
able clock.   How can I ever convey to others an
idea of the comfort and consolation that this old

clock has been for years to me! . . . What other
thing that has not life could cheer me as it does!
what other thing that has not life (I will not say
how few things that have) has proved the same
patient, true, untiring friend! How often have I
sat in the long winter evenings feeling society in its
cricket voice! how often in the summer twilight,
when my thoughts have wandered back to a melan-
choly past, have its regular whisperings recalled them
to the calm and peaceful present! how often, in the
dead tranquillity of night, has its bell broken the op-
pressive silence, and seemed to give me assurance that
the old clock was still on guard at my chamber-door!'

The Hall clock is often a plain, simple, un-
decorated instrument, where all others are perhaps
somewhat ornamented. Bracket clocks for the staircase or landings, Mantelpiece clocks for the drawing and dining rooms, for the study, the boudoir,
and the best bed rooms, have each their separate shape
and character specially designed, and are to be found
in simple black-stained wood or real ebony, in marble
of different colours, in bronze, in buhl, and in ormolu, with or without enamel ornaments, and with
or without miniature figures at base, sides, and top.
Until lately most of our ornamental mantelpiece
clocks were imported from the continent, although
French workmanship is generally inferior to our
own, but preference was shown by the public to the

former on account of the greater attention given by
the French to external decorations and variety of
pattern. I am endeavouring to provide that for the
future this branch of clockmaking shall not be aban-
boned entirely to our continental neighbours, whose
exports of this kind to our country yearly are very
considerable. Henceforth by means of new designs
specially made for me and by me, and of a sufficiently
skilled staff of artistic workmen, selected for the purpose of working under my superintendence, on my
own premises, I shall be able to compete on equal,
nay, as to mechanism, on superior, terms with the
best specimens of decorated clocks from foreign atéli-
ers. There is no reason why the admitted superiority
of English mechanism should not be coupled with
the best designs for decorated clock-cases; there is
every reason why handsome clocks should be made
which will keep time well, and add not only by their
beauty but their usefulness to the enjoyment of
domestic life. If the proverb, 'handsome is that
handsome does,' applies to clocks, English workmanship should soon obtain pre-eminence, for it is well
known that the principle upon which French clocks
are generally made renders them less durable time-
pieces.

The most ancient clocks differed in many respects
from those now in use. Clocks of the earlier period
had, as we have said, instead of the pendulum now

in use, a *balance*, vibrating on the top of the clock, as the regulating medium. The escapement was of the verge construction, a sketch of which will be seen below, which represents a clock of a most ancient character.

Without entering into any very minute detail of

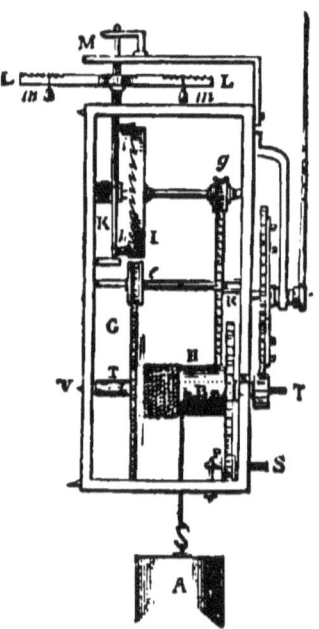

Old Balance-Clock.

the manner in which motion in a clock is successively communicated from one toothed wheel (G or R) or pinion (*e* or *g*) to another, which, indeed, would only tend to perplex the mind of the general reader, it will be sufficient to state the following. s is a square piece of steel fixed to and forming part of the pinion P. In winding the clock the key is placed upon this square, and being turned round continuously in one direction, the pinion P turns with it. This communicates its motion to the wheel R, which is fixed to the cylinder B, and which in its revolution coils or winds up the cord to which is attached the weight A. While this takes place the wheel G is held in check by another wheel, called the 'ratchet,' and a click (neither of which is seen in the sketch), but when the operation of the winding is completed, and the weight A begins to descend, the cylinder B, together with the wheel G, turn on their common pivots V, V, and the motion is thus communicated from wheel to pinion until it reaches the escapement-wheel I. The teeth of this wheel, in its revolution, act alternately on the pallets *i, h*, which project from and form part of the spindle or verge K, M, and thus produce a vibratory or backward and forward motion of the balance L, L.

Were it not for this detention, the duration of which is much increased by the swing of the balance, the weight A would descend with gradually accelerated speed, till, in a few moments, the cord would be entirely unwound from the cylinder, and the clock be at rest.

The SPRING CLOCK as ordinarily made is thus constructed. The frame consists of two oblong plates of brass pinned together by short pillars, and pierced with holes, in which run the arbors of the various wheels. Next, the mainspring, the moving or motive power of the clock, which is a riband of steel, highly tempered, and enclosed in a cylinder or barrel. In the middle of this barrel is the spring or barrel arbor, to which the spring is hooked at one end, the other end being fixed to the circum-

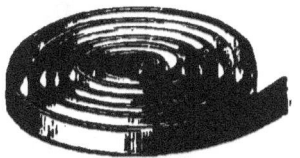

Clock Spring.

ference of the barrel. Outside the frame or plate,
and at the end of the arbor, is the ratchet, a wheel
with saw-like teeth. This is acted upon by a click,
which, falling into the ratchet teeth, prevents the
recoil of the mainspring, so that the spring has no
means of uncoiling itself, except by the moving of
the train of wheels. This click is screwed to the outside of the oblong plate. The power of the mainspring is transmitted to the train of wheels by means
of a chain or gut, one end of which is fastened to the
outer edge of the barrel, and the other end to the
fusee, which is of conical shape, securely fastened to
the arbor or axis of the main wheel; on this same
arbor is the square, on which the key is put for winding. When this square is turned in winding, the
fusee draws the chain or gut from off the outer edge
of the barrel, and coils up the spring within it. The
spring when fully wound, and consequently at its
greatest power, acts by means of the chain or gut
on the small end of the fusee, which in turning
drives the train of wheels. As the spring becomes
gradually uncoiled, and the power exerted less, the
leverage is increased in the same proportion by the
increased width of the fusee on which it acts.

To prevent the straining of the spring, a little
contrivance called the stop-work is introduced. It
consists of a piece of steel somewhat in the shape of
a bayonet, which is so fixed and contrived that the

last turn of the gut or chain on the fusee forces the stop into contact with a projection on the end of the fusee, which abutting against it, forms the check felt when the clock is wound up. On the same arbor with the fusee is fixed the main wheel, which with the before-described contrivance of click and ratchet, ·permits the turning of the fusee or winding-up of the clock, while it itself remains stationary. This wheel acts in the centre pinion (a pinion is a little wheel playing in the teeth of a larger wheel, and has six, eight, ten, or twelve teeth, or, as they are called, leaves), which is fixed to the centre arbor, and carries the minute hand. This pinion is so constructed in relation to the other parts of the clock as to make one revolution in an hour; the centre wheel being firmly riveted on the pinion, it must also revolve once an hour. The centre wheel acts into another pinion, which is called the third wheel pinion, upon the arbor or axle of which is securely fixed the third wheel, which again acts in the escape-pinion carrying the escapement-wheel. On the top of the back plate is firmly screwed the back cock, or the support of the pendulum; which is suspended from it by a flexible spring, as before described. This pendulum receives impulsion from the wheel-work by means of the crutch, a small part attached to the arbor of the pallets, and which projects downwards about three inches, parallel with the pendulum rod. To the lower part of the crutch is screwed or riveted at a right angle a piece of steel, in such a direction as to penetrate the pendulum rod, which has a slot or hole cut to receive it; impulsion is thus given to the pendulum. Between the frame and dial-plate is the motion work, consisting of three wheels; the first, called the minute wheel, is attached to the arbor of the centre wheel, which, it will be recollected, makes one revolution an hour, and acts in a wheel of the same size, whose axle carries a pinion serving to drive the hour wheel. This hour wheel is supported by a bridge screwed over the minute wheel. The dial is pinned on to the front plate; the hour hand is fixed on a socket communicating with the hour wheel, and the minute hand on the arbor of the centre wheel.

When a clock is intended to strike, a separate train of wheels has to be introduced into it,—one train of wheels serving to keep the time, and another train for the striking part. It may be as well to add that a greater amount of labour is required to make the striking than the going part of a clock.

There are only two kinds of striking parts now in use, and these are characterized by the terms 'Rack' striking work, and 'Count-wheel,' or 'Locking-plate,' striking work. The Rack striking work (see next page) is the best and safest ever introduced, because with it the clock may be made to strike any number of times within the hour. A, the minute wheel revolving in the direction of the arrow, and driving the wheel B, which is of the same size, and has the same number of teeth. C, a pin fixed in the wheel B, and acting on the lever D, which has its centre of motion in the point E. L, the click, the lower point of which acts in the teeth K of the rack M.

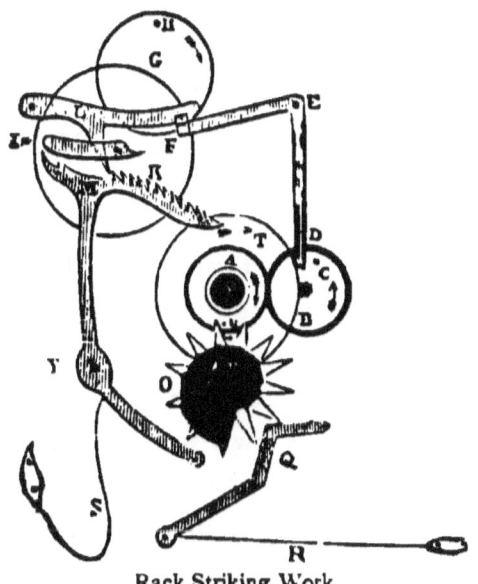

Rack Striking Work.

S, the rack-spring, which acts upon the lower end of the rack, or, as it is called, the rack-tail, and brings it in contact with the snail P. Q and R are the jumper and its spring, by which the snail P, fastened to the star-wheel O, is kept in its place. Y, the centre of motion of the rack, on which it acts freely. In the wheel A is fixed a pin U, which, as the wheel A rotates, gradually forces before it a tooth of the star-wheel O,

8

which carries with it the snail P, until at last the
second step of the snail is opposite the rack-tail.
While this is going on, the wheel B, driven by the
wheel A, is advancing in the opposite direction, and,
by means of the pin C, is pushing before it the end of
the lever D. It is obvious that the other end, F, of
the lever will be gradually raised, and this will lift the
lower point of the click L out of the teeth of the rack.
The latter being now free will yield to the action of
the spring s, which will force its lower end into contact with the second step of the snail, and throw back
the head of the rack to a corresponding extent. By
this action the striking train of wheels is released, and
the two wheels, G and I, seen in the upper part of our
cut, begin to rotate, but are stopped by H, a pin
that is caught by a stud which projects from the
end F of the lever. As the wheel B advances, the pin
c gradually frees itself from the long arm of the lever
D, which drops by its own weight into its original
position, and frees the wheels G and I, which immediately commence once more to rotate. At the
centre of the wheel I is fixed the gathering pallet,
that, as it revolves with the wheel, gathers up one
by one the teeth of the rack, which is prevented from
falling back by the lower end of the click L, and thus
gradually draws it forward until the last tooth is
reached, when the end of the gathering pallet abuts
on the end of the rack head, and the train of wheels

is once more at rest.　It is obvious that for every
tooth of the rack which is gathered up, there is one
revolution of the wheel 1, and this communicates
with the tail of the hammer, causing at each revolution a blow on the bell.　There is, as will be at once
seen, an important connection between the various
parts.　When the second step of the snail is presented
to the rack-tail, the head of the rack is thrown back
a distance corresponding to the width of two of its
teeth.　This requires two revolutions of the gathering
pallet to return it to its place; and these two revolutions of the pallet and the wheel which carries it
govern the two blows on the bell which signify the
hour.　At three o'clock the third step of the snail
will be presented to the hammer-tail, and so on.

On the next page is an illustration of the back part
of a French Clock, as seen upon opening the door of
the case.　At the right hand side will be observed the
count-wheel A, fitting tightly upon a prolonged square
arbor of the second wheel in the train, and having
twelve openings of unequal length around its outer
edge, 1, 2, &c.　Just above the wheel towards the right
will also be seen the 'Dog,' or 'Detent,' F, which
falls into these notches, and is a part of the locking
similar to that which is represented at the stud and
the pin H.　So soon as the stud is lifted the pin
becomes disengaged, the wheel-work revolves, and
the count-wheel being firmly fixed to the prolonged

arbor of one of those wheels, advances with it
in the direction indicated by the arrow, the detent

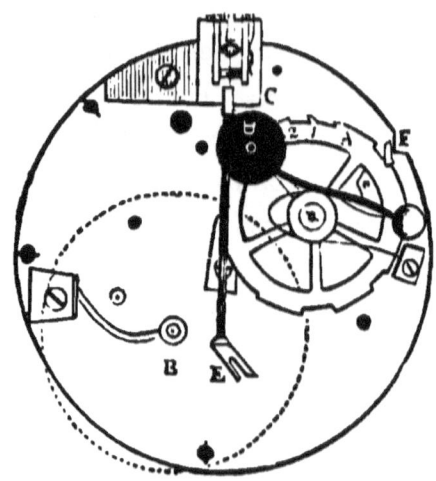

Back of French Clock.

resting upon the plain part of the locking-wheel.
When the required number of hours have struck,
the notch approaches the detent, the gravity of which
allows it to fall therein.

In connection with this detent is also another
projecting piece, which is carried inside the frame,
and when it falls presents a broad surface to a pin
fixed in the rim of one of the wheels. Thus the
motion of the wheel-work is stayed until this piece is
again lifted by the going parts from the pin, and held
in that position by the outer rim of the locking-wheel
A, until again the next notch is presented to the
detent. When it falls, the stud is carried with it,

against which the pin becomes engaged. The number of strokes depends on the distance which the
count-wheel has to revolve before being stopped by
the detent F. The chief objection to the locking-
plate being used for striking, arises from the fact that,
if ever the clock is allowed to run down, or if the
clock gets otherwise stopped, it strikes wrong afterwards, until it has been properly re-set to the hour.

Clocks are made of all manner of shapes, patterns,
and sizes, for all manner of places, positions, and
persons.

BRACKET CLOCKS, which are intended to occupy
but a small space, say on a staircase, or lobby, or land-
ing, are sometimes made with extreme finish, care, and
elegance, sometimes are simply plain and devoid of
embellishment. They are constructed with or without striking work.

CHIME CLOCKS are a great addition to the attrac-
tions of a house. They are usually made to go eight
or fifteen days; to strike the hours and quarters on
four or eight bells or gongs.

MUSICAL CLOCKS are constructed so as to play
several tunes at certain intervals with the greatest
finish and perfection. The mechanism for time-
keeping being easily disconnected from the musical
mechanism, the latter may be stopped without any
interference with the clock as a time-keeper.

CARRIAGE CLOCKS are made so as to be un-

affected by the motion of the vehicle. They are
usually of a small and squarish shape, enclosed in

Carriage Clock.

leather, so as to protect the case from scratches; but
they vary in size,—measuring usually from four to
seven inches high by two-and-a-half to four inches in
breadth and the same in depth. Some are made
without striking movement, some to strike hours,
half-hours, and quarters, some with repeating work,
and some with an alarm added to them.

LIBRARY and DINING-ROOM CLOCKS are frequently seen decorated with highly elegant ornaments,
in bronze, marble, ormolu, and with miniature figures,
as well as objects of still life, but these clocks are

usually not so conspicuously ornamental as those
which are designed for the drawing-room.

SKELETON CLOCKS are so named from their
movements being all bare and uncovered. When
watches were comparative novelties it was not at all
an uncommon desire on the part of their possessors
to watch the operations of a mechanism which was
regarded as wonderfully resembling life itself. Watch
cases were consequently made of crystal, and were
found strong and serviceable. In skeleton clocks the
escapement is sometimes made a peculiarly interesting
feature to the non-professional eye delighting in
noting the amazing accuracy with which each piece
of the mechanism works and combines to produce the
result required.

REGULATOR CLOCKS are, as we have said, the most
perfect time-pieces which can be manufactured.

TELL-TALE CLOCKS are of great service in secur-
ing the attention and watchfulness of persons left in
care of premises or property. They are made with a
number of pins projecting round the edge of the dial,
and coming into contact once every quarter of an
hour with a pin fixed at the top part of the dial, over
the part which in an ordinary clock is occupied by XII.
The dial revolves completely once every twelve
hours, and presents one of the projecting pins to the
index every quarter of an hour; the watchman should
then be ready at hand to pull a cord, by means of

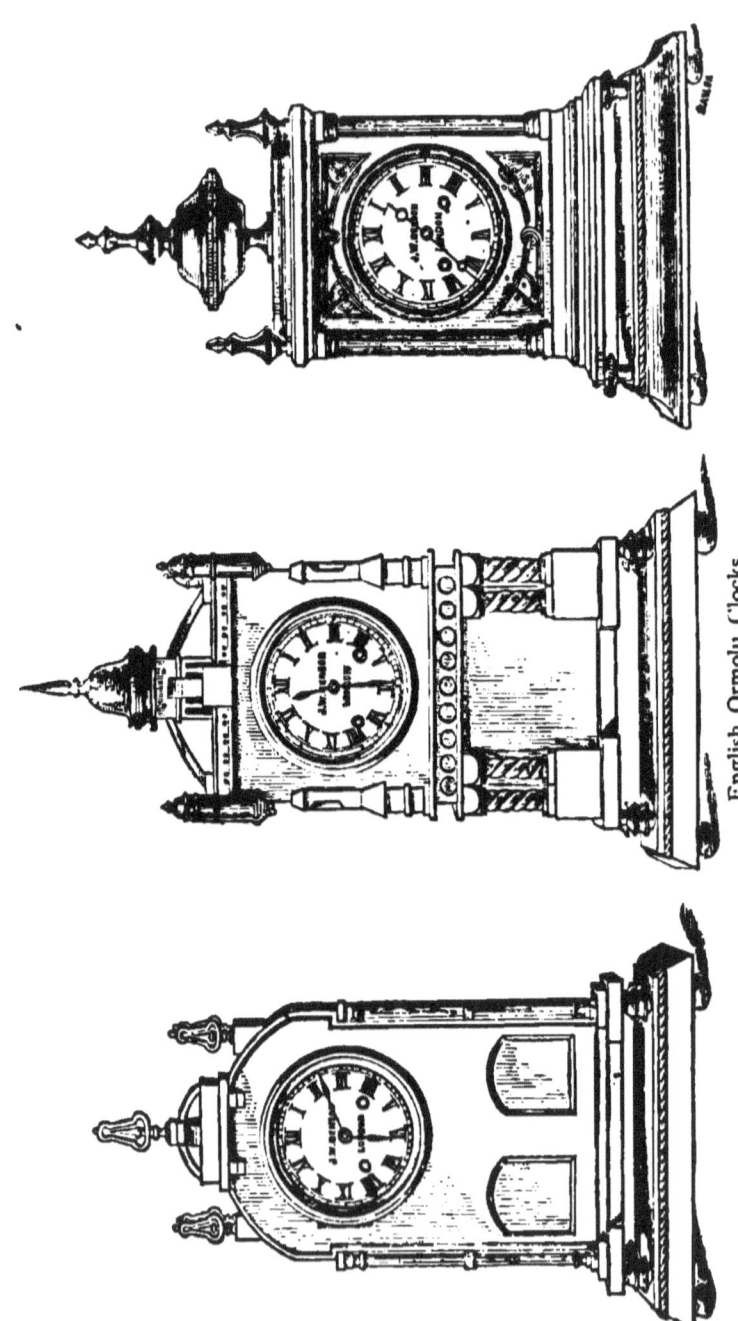

English Ormolu Clocks.

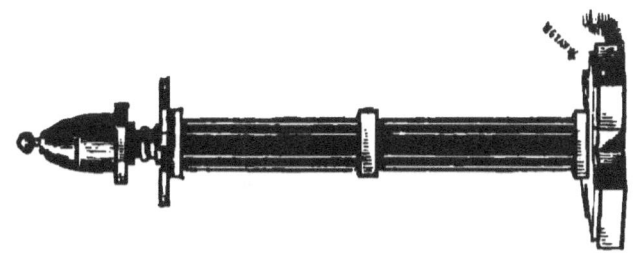

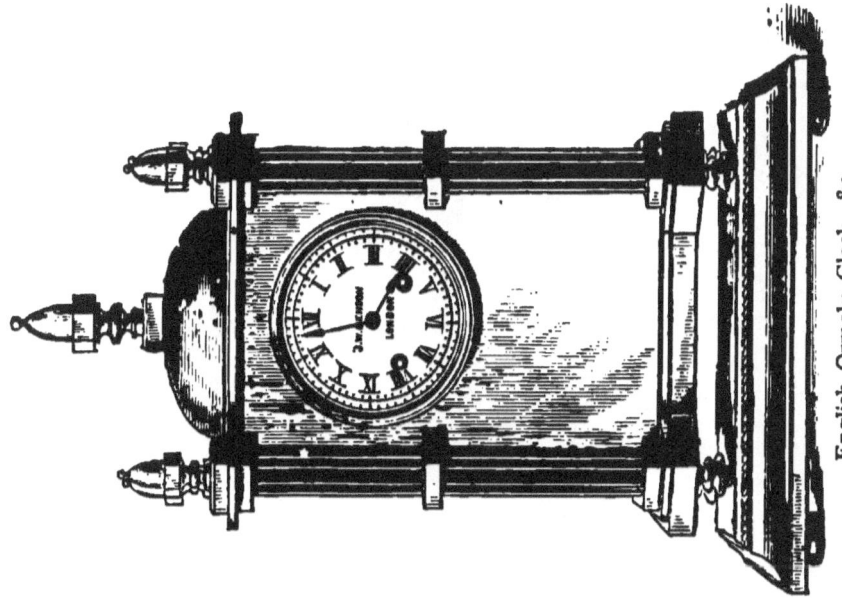

English Ormolu Clock, &c.

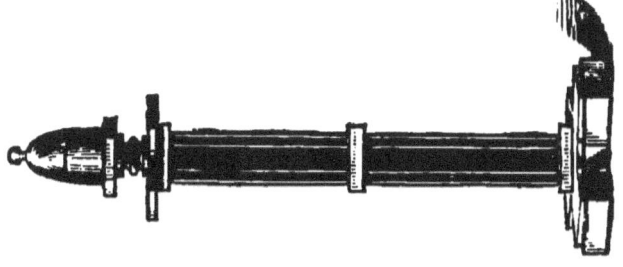

English Ormolu Clock, &c.

which the projecting pin is pushed in; otherwise the

Tell-Tale Clock.

dial shows the exact time of his absence and neglect of duty.

ELECTRICAL CLOCKS have been several times planned and made by different ingenious inventors, and obtained considerable notice, but they have not been hitherto as successful as was expected. Electricity has been applied to the direct movement of the pendulum itself, and subsequently to the raising a small weight to act upon the pendulum in the style of a gravity escapement. In perhaps the latest of these instruments, called a Magnetic Clock, an electromagnet was used to relieve the pendulum from the

influence of the spring by which impulsion had been
given, and to make the return or reflex vibration.
Electric clocks are now seldom made; electric dials
without any clock-movement in connection with them
are made to show the standard time by means of a
galvanic current sent from the Greenwich Observatory
clock at intervals of a minute or half-minute it may
be,—even as Electric Timeballs show to distant towns
and out-ports, by means of such a current, the exact
Greenwich time once a day.

The ELECTRO-CHRONOGRAPH is a new and useful
invention for timing with great precision the quickest
of events. It is applied to a central seconds clock
with a dial three feet in circumference showing the
hours, minutes, seconds and fifths of seconds. This
clock erected in a prominent position, say on a race-
ground, and worked by electricity enables the starter
of a race to set the works in motion; by means of a
tape held up at the winning post and connected with
the batteries, the winner upon breasting the tape stops
the hand of the clock.

The following simple directions will be found of
great use in the management of a Clock :—

When the Clock is unpacked it should be carefully
handled with a silk handkerchief or piece of tissue
paper, to prevent the moisture of the hands soiling
the case. Unscrew the bell and take it off, then

put on the pendulum by passing it through the fork, and hang it upon the two small brass pins, *with the hook from you.* Screw on the bell with the convex part outwards, taking care that it does not touch the pendulum.

The stand or bracket should be both steady and level before the Clock is placed upon it; for, unless the Clock is quite in proper beat—that is, unless the beats or ticks occur at equal intervals, it cannot go regularly.

In order to set the Clock to the hour of the day, the minute-hand should be turned on carefully forward with the finger and thumb, the setter pausing as he reaches the XII. and the VI., to allow the Clock to strike each hour and half-hour.

If the striking should at any time be wrong, and it should strike the hour at the half-hour, or the half-hour at the hour, the error can be rectified by moving the minute-hand on to 5 minutes before the hour, or half-hour, and then back until it strikes.

Or, if it should strike a wrong hour—*e.g.*, supposing the Clock should strike 3, and the hour-hand point at 7, then the hour-hand may be moved back to 3, and the Clock afterwards set to the hour of the day in the usual manner.

If, at any future time, the Clock should require regulating, the small steel square above the XII. is the regulator, and turning it a *little* to the right (half-turn of key) will make the Clock go faster, and to the left, slower.   This should be repeated until the desired effect is obtained.

The bell-stud, or arm to which the bell is screwed, is purposely made of soft metal, so that it can be bent up or down so as to obtain a heavy or light blow of the hammer as may be desired.

Both squares in the dial should be wound once a week.

TURRET CLOCKS.

A CHURCH tower without a clock and bells seems
an unfurnished edifice, which must be fitted and filled
before it can serve the purpose for which it was built;
—like a form without life, a body without a soul. A
good Church clock is useful to everybody; it is the
friendly monitor alike of rich and poor,—the regulator
of every private time-piece,—the standard of time for
a whole parish or township. By it the artisan or
mechanic trudges off to his daily labour; by it the
tradesman opens and closes his shop; by it the school-
boy is admonished as 'with shining morning face he
creeps like snail unwillingly to school;' by it the law
itself regulates its penalties,—(enacting, as it does,
house-breaking between nine at night and six in the
morning to be the heavier crime of burglary;)—by it,
in a word, are all the multifarious transactions of every-
day life more or less regulated and measured, and when
the church clock stops, it produces a social discomfort
and anarchy throughout a whole neighbourhood, to
an extent scarcely credible. A good public clock is a

benefit to all,—a faulty one is a general nuisance and
a continual source of irritation.   A public clock is in
its way as necessary as the public highway, the public
market, the public law itself.   It is the product and
the symbol of advanced civilization, the one ever-
wakeful watchman and trusty friend of all, by whose
chimes the sleepless merchant has often planned his
ventures   or   sighed o'er   apprehended   losses   and
dangers; the student busied with researches has con-
sumed the midnight oil; the sick have counted their
hours of pain, longing in the night for the dawn, in
the daytime for the night.   On the other hand, when
one like Mr Justice Shallow is reminded of the mad
days of his London youth, he very aptly associates
them with the Bacchanalian memories which Falstaff
appeals to,—'We have heard the chimes at midnight.'

To have lived ' where bells have knoll'd to church '
was according to Shakspere to have been blessed by
humanizing influences comparable with those produced by having—

> ' Sat at good men's feasts, and wiped our eyes
> Of drops that sacred pity has engendered.'

Cowper can find no better words to describe the utter
desolation of the island where the shipwrecked Selkirk
bemoaned his absolute solitude ' out of humanity's
reach,' than by putting into his mouth the language—

'But the sound of a church-going bell
These valleys and rocks never heard,
Never sigh'd at the sound of a knell,
Nor smiled when a Sabbath appear'd.'

In our every-day experience we can each testify
to the truthfulness of the poet who points to the close
association which exists in most minds between the
church clock and the varying times and seasons, with
their different joys and sorrows, and we can most of
us say, with Southey,—

'I love the bell that calls the poor to pray,
    Chiming from village church its cheerful sound,
When the sun smiles on labour's holy-day
    And all the rustic train are gather'd round,
Each deftly dizen'd in his Sunday's best,
And pleased to hail the day of piety and rest.

And when, dim shadowing o'er the face of day,
    The mantling mists of eventide rise slow,
As through the forest gloom I wend my way,
    The minster curfew's sullen voice I know,
And pause, and love its solemn toll to hear,
As made by distance soft it dies upon the ear.'

It is but a short step from the sentimental consideration of such reminiscences to the practical inquiry
how is the public time kept, and yet it is one which
probably is seldom taken with a view to more or less
thorough investigation. Without traversing the distance which divides us from that antique time when
Archimedes measured the shadows of the Pyramids

9

by his walking-stick, or when the 'dial of Ahaz' was constructed as one of the first of historical time-measurers, we can discover the principles upon which an instrument such as a thoroughly serviceable public clock of the present time, with all the newest improvements both in time-keeping and in wearing qualities, should be produced.

It is of some consequence, in the first place, to know that the introduction of steam-machinery has added to the accuracy of clock-work and at the same time considerably diminished its cost; fifty or sixty years ago there would have been charged as much as £800 for a turret clock inferior to that which may now be procured for £150; and the result is to be seen in the largely increased numbers of public time-pieces. It is obvious, however, that there is none the less need of care in the choice of a Clock-maker, for upon his skill and trustworthiness will depend whether the money be well spent or not, and whether the instrument furnished by him prove to be valuable and serviceable. It is not a purchase wherein the buyer can usually of himself judge of the merits of his bargain, he must rely upon the reputation established by previous works of the same kind. If the Clock-maker be not merely a clock-seller (as is too often the case, for Turret Clock-makers are but few), he will be able to point to similar instruments made and set up by himself in different towns and cities, in proof

of his ability, but there will still be a necessity for ex-
plaining to the purchaser the chief points upon which
the accuracy of such a time-keeper must depend.

In the first place, it is necessary to say that Turret
Clocks are not merely house clocks upon an enlarged
scale, differing from the latter merely in size and
weight, but that the extra strength of the machinery
requires greater weight of materials 'in a ratio as
much higher as the cube is higher than the square of
any of its dimensions,' and that increased weight
means increase of friction.   Besides this point which
is peculiarly the province of the Turret Clock-maker,
there are important questions to be considered by
architects and their employers as to the proper method
of constructing a Turret Clock chamber, so as to
prevent too much atmospheric variation,—heat and
cold, wind and damp, being each likely in some degree, as the seasons change, to affect the public time-
keeper,—as witness the clock of St Paul's Cathedral,
popularly believed to be an exemplary piece of mechanism, and yet often forced by the wind to vary its time
so as to damage its own reputation among those who
narrowly watch its behaviour under what may be
called trying circumstances.   It is not wise to build a
tower without careful consideration for the tenant
which is to occupy it, or having regard merely to
architectural notions of external proportion, for usually
it happens that when clock and bells occur as an after-

thought, there is often some difficulty and extra expense in planning the room for them. Plenty of
length and breadth to allow of the proper fall of the
clock-weights and the swing of the pendulum save
much in the cost of fixing, and are necessary to secure
good time-keeping with the least trouble, for it is obvious that where numerous bevelled wheels with rod-
work are employed for the purpose of moving the hands
over the dial, if the probabilities of unvarying accuracy
are not lessened, the cost must be much increased.
Works which have to be placed at some distance from
the dials must be more powerful than if they could
be put in their proper place, and a little forethought
in the architect will save much money both in the
original price of the machinery of a clock and in its
subsequent repair. Then again, there is always the
question for and against the illumination of dials to
be considered, and of course with this is unavoidably
mixed up not only the arrangements as regards space
for the proper working of the time-keeping, striking,
and lighting machinery, but the vexed question of
ventilation above referred to, — some horologers
asserting that chambers as nearly air tight as may be
should be devised, and others that there ought to be a
draught through the clock-room. There are in fact
so many opinions more or less excellent, according
to the circumstances of each case, that there is no
laying down any arbitrary and unvarying rule,—

much must be left to the discretion of the Turret
Clock manufacturer,—upon whom as has been already
stated it is necessary also to rely for the essentials of
a good clock, viz., the soundness of the materials,
the quality of the workmanship, and the scientific
accuracy with which the instrument has been planned
and put together. Now before considering the present advanced state of the art of Turret Clock-making
and the various improvements which have to be carefully studied and applied by the makers who would
bear the highest reputations as manufacturers, it
will be necessary to bear in mind what has been said
of the step-by-step progress in horological science of
which we have already endeavoured to give the
chief particulars. From 1288 A.D., the date of the
oldest historical clock — that mentioned as having
been set up near Westminster Hall by means of
funds derived from a fine levied by the Lord Chief
Justice of the period — till now when Big Ben
reigns in its stead, is a long interval, with many
wonderful incidents, and some great historical names.
Henry de Wyck's Paris invention, Galileo's discovery
of the pendulum, Huygens's practical application
of that discovery, Dr Hooke's ' anchor ' escapement,
and Graham's dead-beat escapement, Harrison's
' gridiron ' pendulum, and the latest applications of
electricity and eccentricity, have each and all their
peculiar attraction for horological students, but we

need not recur to these branches of this highly interesting subject elsewhere treated of. We will proceed to mention a few memoranda about several old
public clocks whose ingenious mechanism gained for
them a well-deserved fame,—not, perhaps, so much for
accuracy in time-keeping as for the grotesque devices
with which old clock-makers amused their cotempor-
aries. To them time, as such, was perhaps of not so
much consequence as it is to us in these days of tele-
graph and steam communication. We moderns seem
to think it a task sufficiently difficult to set up a sound
public time-piece without connecting therewith the
wonder-working machinery of a wax-work exhibition.

The CLOCK AT WELLS CATHEDRAL, made originally A.D. 1340, by a monk named Peter Lightfoot, is
one of the best known of its class still in some sort
of working order. The dial of this horologe is divided
into 24 hours; it shows the motion of the sun and
moon, and bears upon its summit eight armed knights
on horseback, tilting with lance in rest at one another,
by a double rotatory motion. This clock was removed
from Glastonbury to Wells after the dissolution of
the Glastonbury Monastery. In 1835 the works
were so worn away that they were replaced by a new
train, the curious old dial and equestrian knights
being still retained.

ST DUNSTAN's CLOCK [see p. 137]. This Clock,
when old St Dunstan's Church in Fleet Street was

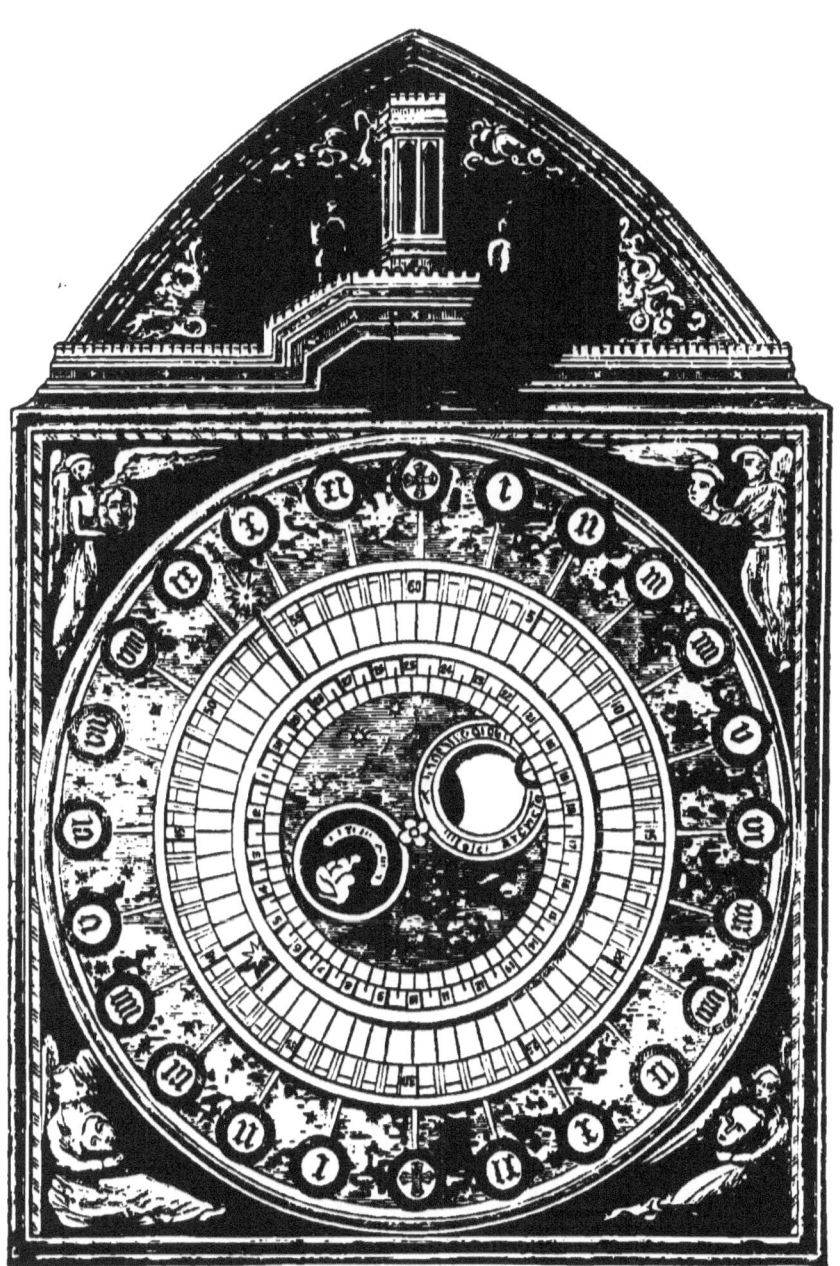

Wells Cathedral Clock.

pulled down, was sold by public auction, and bought
by the late Marquis of Hertford, for whom Decimus
Burton the architect erected St Dunstan's Villa in the
Regent's Park.   In the grounds of that villa this old
clock with its automaton giants striking the hours
and quarters was put up, and it is there still, to be seen
in full working order, performing the same duties as
of yore in Fleet Street.

ST JAMES'S PALACE CLOCK [see p. 138] is one of
the most ancient public time-pieces now in use, but is
intended soon to be removed it is said to South Kensington Museum.   It has a locking-plate with ting-
tang quarter, the quarter hammers being raised from
the pin wheel while the striking hammer is lifted from
the pins in the main wheel.   It has a crown-wheel
escapement with teeth on its edge, and the pallets
working upright instead of over the top like a verge
escapement.   The hands are connected by the bevel
wheels below the clock.   The whole of the going
train with the intermediate and bevel wheels are
attached to the one bar so that the whole of the works
have to be removed if one piece requires alteration or
renewal.   The pendulum rod is of iron.

ST PAUL'S CATHEDRAL CLOCK [see p. 140] is one
of the best examples of old-fashioned clocks in London; it occupies the clock-room in the south-western
tower.   It may be described as a ting-tang quarter on
the rack principle, having hammers raised from pins in

St Dunstan's Clock.

the main wheel as in St James's Palace Clock.   The
train is run in a bar, so that to get away one piece
the rest must be disturbed.   The escapement is a

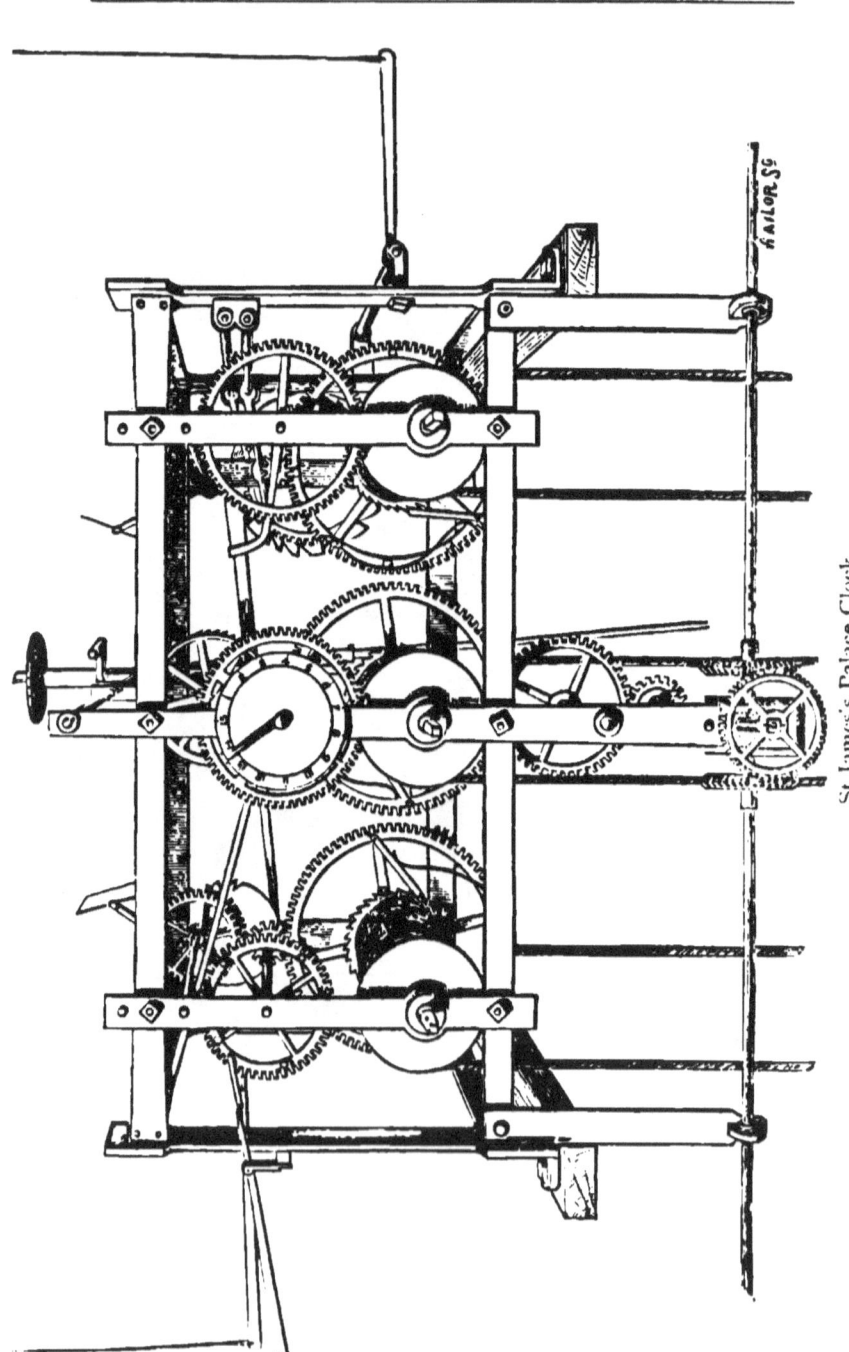

St James's Palace Clock.

recoil, beating two seconds with a wood rod pendulum. The length of the minute hand is eight feet, and its weight 75℔; the length of the hour hand is five feet five inches, and its weight 44℔. The diameter of the bell, made from old 'Great Tom of Westminster,' is about 10 feet, its weight 11,474℔; the hammer weighs -145℔, and the clapper 180℔.

The OLD CLOCK AT THE ROYAL FREE HOSPITAL, GRAY'S INN LANE, is a fair specimen of the work of 120 years ago. It has a recoil escapement, most of the wheels are of wrought-iron, cut by hand, as is also the pinion. The pendulum rod is of iron with leaden bob.

THE WHEELS.

And now, in order to form a judgment of what is necessary to be done to make a really sound and valuable Turret Clock of the present day, let me describe the materials of which it should be formed. One of the most important parts of a clock is the wheel-work. Iron wheels are of course very much cheaper than those which are made of gun metal or hard brass, but iron wheels, however well they may sometimes wear, are more liable to oxidize and to decay, and although it is certain that a large number of clocks are constructed with iron wheels by London houses of some reputation, a few years are generally sufficient to prove

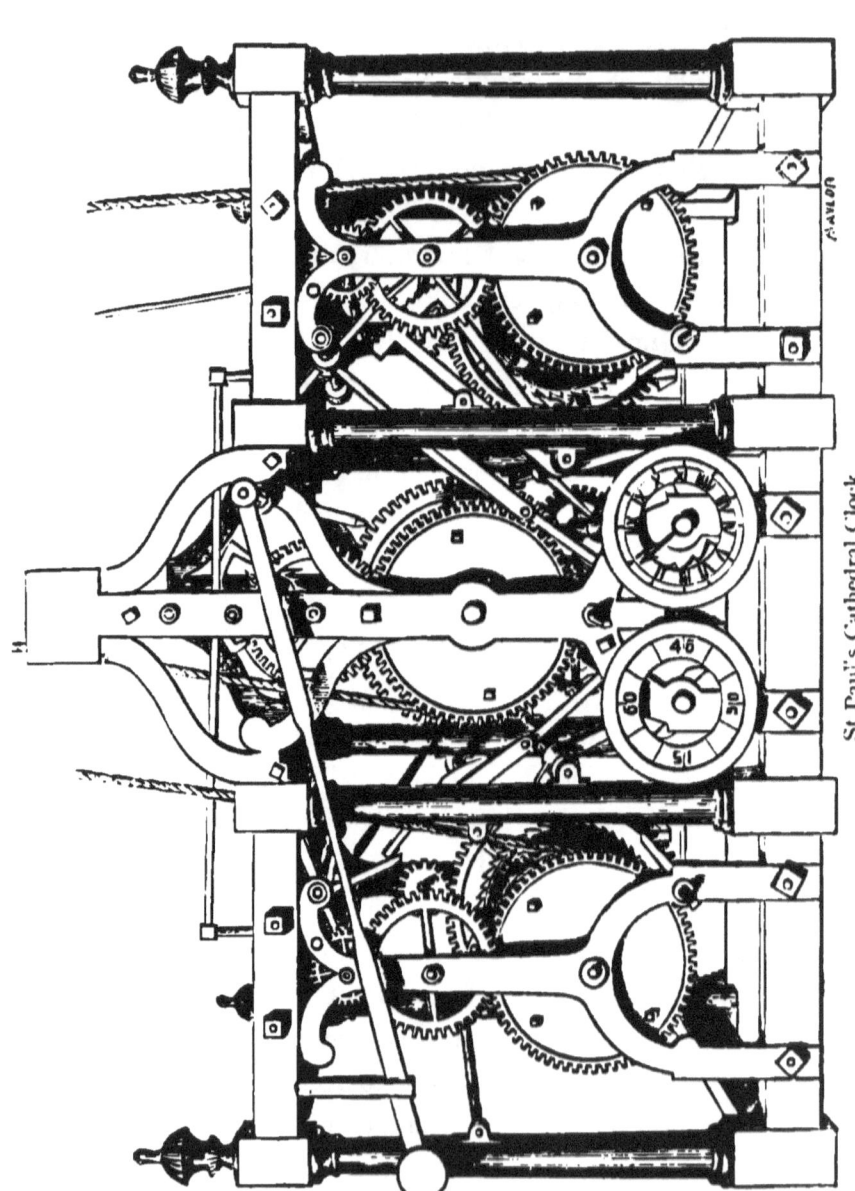

St Paul's Cathedral Clock.

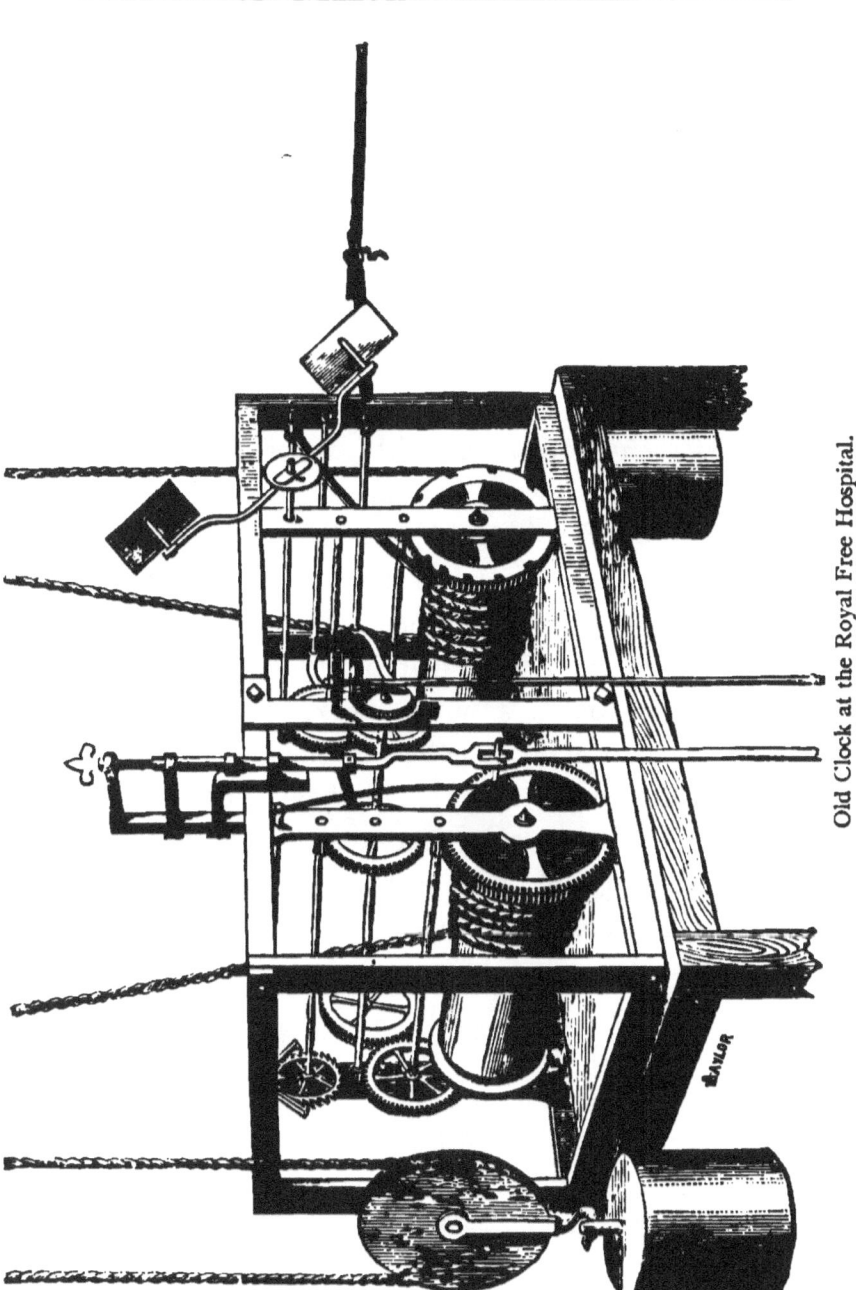

Old Clock at the Royal Free Hospital.

such time-pieces to be very faulty, and to necessitate the substitution of wheels of the superior metal.

The best clocks are usually made with wheels of the best gun metal. The teeth are cut by steam power, with an improved cutting engine; and at the same moment that the teeth are cut, they are finished by the engine without the aid of the file, sand-paper, or other polishing materials, so that the most minute difference cannot possibly occur, their accuracy being secured even to the thousandth part of an inch. In the old times this work was done by a man turning a fly-wheel, but that method necessarily occasioned an unevenness of cut which had afterwards to be removed by filing and hand polishing. Wheels thus made could not of course have that precision of movement which is essential in a public clock, and which can only be obtained by a perfect mechanical fit of the teeth of the wheels, such true mechanical fitting being only secured by truly accurate cutting machines. Hand cutting varies with each artisan, and therefore cannot be equally trustworthy. In cheap clocks, constructed to suit public companies who give their contract to the lowest tender, iron is frequently used instead of steel, both in the pinions and arbors, and cast-iron takes the place of gun metal or hard brass in the wheels and bosses,—the result usually being that the Public Clock gets into disrepute through its requiring to be repaired so frequently, and more money

is expended upon such repairs than would have sufficed
for the purchase of a thoroughly perfect time-keeper.
It is urged by the advocates of iron wheels that a
clock can be manufactured at a considerably less
cost by their employment, but in estimating expense
there seems to have been overlooked the important
question, as to what will be the probable durability
of the machine.

I should be sorry to condemn wholesale all clocks,
the main wheels of which are made of iron, but very
certain it is that a large proportion of clocks constructed of this material and by London houses of
great reputation (despite of their possessing an
escapement invented by amateurs who consider themselves the depositories of all horological knowledge),
have been found most faulty time-keepers, and after
a few years have become entirely worn out and useless.

It is argued (and rightly so) by the advocates of
iron wheels that case-hardened pinions should not be
used, in consequence of their wearing with great unevenness, but such persons should be reminded that
this objection is much greater in the instance of cast-
iron wheels. A case came under my notice some
time since of a clock made by a London house, with
iron wheels, which after comparatively little time became entirely worn out and had to be removed, a
result not at all surprising to those who are aware

of the porous nature of iron. The TEETH OF
WHEELS have to be made with the greatest skill
and care in order that the entire mechanism shall
work without friction, and shall not only temporarily keep time with regularity, but shall last for
many years without renewal. Teeth should fit into
one another without a squeezing pressure (which
is equivalent to friction), but with exact uniformity of
contact, the action being almost entirely between the
teeth separating from each other and not between
those which are approaching, *i.e.* in technical language, the action should be after the line of centres
of the wheels and not before it.

Church clocks were accustomed formerly to be
made to go for thirty-four hours, and to be wound up
every day; by the frequency of which winding the
clock could be made to keep time with great accuracy,
for regulating could be attended to as frequently, and
no great variation could well occur in twenty-four
hours. But the regulating, as a matter of course,
requires a regulator, or standard, of time, which is not
always to be found in country places, nor even is the
man in charge of clock-winding always in possession
of a watch sufficiently accurate to convey the time
from the regulator if there were one to the Church
clock. Of late, Church clocks are made to go eight
days, and so the labour of frequent winding has been
saved, while at the same time by extra care in the

manufacture and fixing of a clock, there need be no necessity for frequently regulating it.

PENDULUMS.

Whether the credit of practically applying the mathematical theory and properties of the pendulum was or was not due to Huygens the Dutchman, we have seen that Harris, a London clock-maker, put up the first pendulum clock in St Paul's Church, Covent Garden, in 1621. The great advance upon this discovery was that the pendulum bob must move not in a circle but a cycloid ; and that back and front should be alike both in weight and shape to secure regular vibration. Cylindrical bobs are now in general use for large clocks. The old iron rod pendulums were soon discovered to be affected considerably by variations of heat and cold,—the difference between winter and summer being ascertained to amount to the loss of a minute a week. Harrison's gridiron pendulum was one of the chief endeavours to prevent such variation, followed after a long interval by other ingenious inventions, which gained temporary approval and gradually fell into disuse. Room should be provided by the architect of every clock-tower in the chamber below that containing the movement, to allow of the swing of a 15-feet pendulum.

FALL OF THE WEIGHTS.

We have seen that the position in which a clock is placed in regard to the dial or dials whose hands it is to drive is a matter requiring some attention. Properly the floor of the clock-chamber should be so planned that the clock might stand immediately behind, and level with the dials; for there is extra expense and inconvenience connected with any more distant situation of the works,—the fall of the weights being sometimes difficult in such case to be provided for. The weights should hang, wherever it is possible so to arrange, immediately from the barrel to which they are affixed, without the intervention of pulleys of any kind, and much expense may be saved by providing for the descent of the weights to a considerable depth below the clock-chamber. As an instance however of the extent to which such difficulties can be overcome, I may mention that the hands of my great clock at the International Exhibition were situated nearly 400 feet from the clock-works, while the weights were carried by iron wire ropes over pulleys below the floor to a distance of 200 feet from the movement, then over another pulley fixed at a height of 80 feet from the ground.

The ESCAPEMENT is perhaps the most important part of a clock.

CROWN-WHEEL ESCAPEMENT.

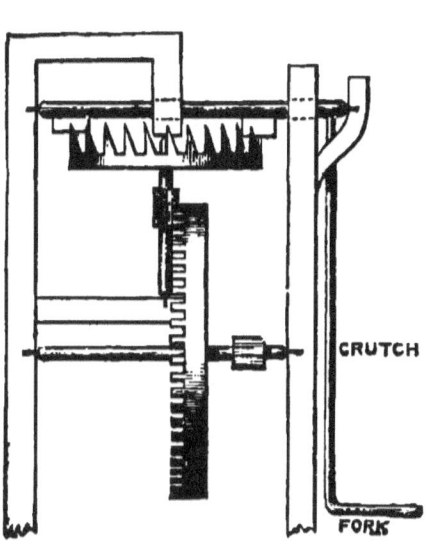

This is the earliest known escapement, and is to be found, as we have said, in Henry de Wyck's clock, all the difference between his escapement and the above being that one of the weights in de Wyck's balance is now set in a vertical instead of a horizontal plane. The bent end or fork seen in the illustration connects the pendulum with that arm technically called the crutch.

THE ANCHOR ESCAPEMENT.

After the crown-wheel escapement, the anchor escapement, invented by Dr Hooke or one of his contemporaries, came into general use, and remains so still; but it is not generally applied to those clocks which are required to go with the nicest accuracy.

In the next illustration the tooth is seen escaping from the left pallet at the moment of the right

pallet's infringing upon the opposite tooth, the pendulum is therefore to be seen still rising a little to the left, and will thus cause the wheel to recoil a little; upon its return the pallet and pendulum are again urged to the right, and so the impulse is continued which is necessary to maintain the motion.

THE DEAD-BEAT ESCAPEMENT

invented by Graham is the one in most general use

for the best clocks made by London makers of the highest repute.

FRENCH SINGLE-PIN ESCAPEMENT.

This is a simple and ingenious escapement (see next page), which after being used for some time

in both France and England went out of use, when,
but recently, it was re-invented by a London watch-

French Single-Pin Escapement.

maker. The teeth are pins of steel set in the face
of the wheel, and the upper half of each cylinder
cut off as well as a small portion of the under or
acting side. This escapement has one great advantage—that if a pin becomes worn or injured it is
easily replaced, whereas in a wheel, if one tooth is
damaged the wheel itself is worthless.

THREE-LEGG'D GRAVITY ESCAPEMENT.

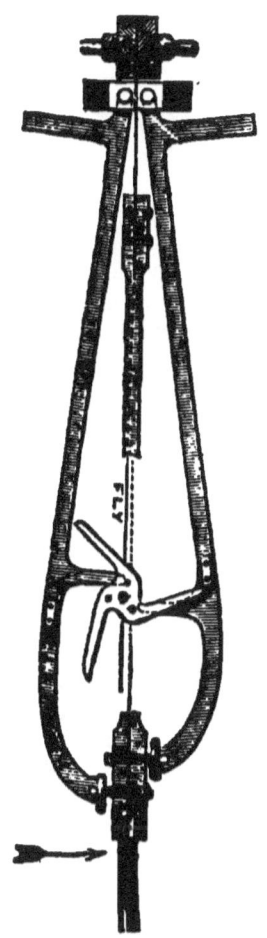

The above illustration represents a regulator escapement as it would appear in a front view; the pallets are lifted by the three central pins. The locking teeth vary in size from one to nearly two inches.   The horizontal pieces projecting from the top of the pallets form the adjustment for the arc of the pendulum.

The great advantages possessed by this escapement over all other gravity escapements, &c., are as follows :—

1. It requires no oil.

2. The angle of the detent planes reduces the friction to almost nil.

3. As the impulse and the unlocking are in one direction, the escapement is unlocked without recoil of impulse arms.

4. No impending force to the pendulum from inertia of impulse arms.

5. The hold in the stops can be increased or diminished to any practical extent by reason of the inverted impulse arms.

6. Less affected by any disturbing forces of the train in proportion to the pressure on the stops.

7. Will bear more weight and give more power to the train without increasing the arc of oscillation.

8. No possibility of tripping under any increase of motive power.

9. The minimum arc of vibration to unlock is 8-tenths of a degree.   Other escapements of similar construction require from 4° to 7°.

10. Take less weight for the motive power in

proportion to the difference of pressure and draught on the lockings.

11. Unlocks by gravitation instead of by the pendulum and at the time of impulse.

12. Requires no fly nor remontoir, and thus reduces the weight of the motive power by one half.

13. The impulse giving motion to the pendulum increases as the force of gravity on the pendulum decreases. A great advantage over those escapements in which the unlocking is done by the pendulum when its momentum is nearly expended and at the extremity of its arc of vibration.

14. The angle of the detent planes can be set so as not only to offer no resistance to the unlocking, but to give an actual impulse in the same manner as the impulse pallets of a dead escapement. This completely frees the impulse which gives motion to the pendulum from any retarding influence of the train.

15. The arc of vibration is more equal in this than in any other gravity escapement.

16. It is not so liable to stop in consequence of a diminution of arc from the variation of motive force in train.

17. It will answer for regulators as well as for turret clocks, its arc of vibration being from 1° to 3°.

DOUBLE THREE-LEGG'D ESCAPEMENT.

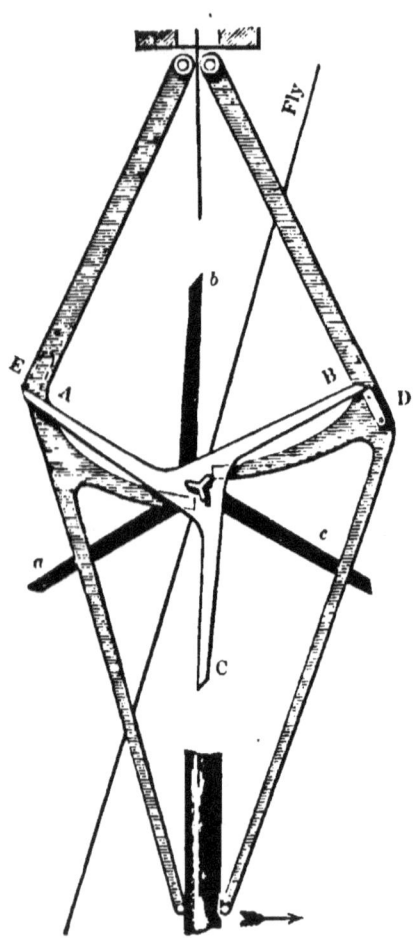

This escapement is chiefly designed for turret-clocks with heavy dial-work requiring much power on the scape-wheel. The peculiarity consists of two locking wheels with one set of lifting pins between them. The wheels are set so that the pallets may lie between, and the pallets fall with the pendulum clear of all other contact. The pallet D for instance has its stop in front for the wheel A B C to act upon, and the E stop is acted upon only by *a b c,* the E and A being on different planes. In this escapement, by making the teeth longer and the pallets shorter, the resistance of the pendulum is much reduced, and the stride of the pallets being wider, the actual weight required of them is considerably lessened,—a point of some importance.

THE REMONTOIRE

is an invention which, being derived from the French, still bears its French title, and consists of either a train remontoire, or a gravity or remontoire escape-ment, in which latter the impulse is not given to the pendulum directly by the clock-train or weight, but by some small weight lifted up or a small spring bent up by the clock-train at every beat of the pendulum, so as to secure a uniform and constant impulse, the remontoire weights being lifted either faster or slower according to need. The train remontoire differs from the escapement but slightly, the chief difference being that the small weight or spring which gives the impulse to the pendulum is not wound up at every beat, but at some larger interval, seldom more than half a minute. Its effect is to counteract the various errors to which large clocks driving heavy hands are always liable, and to diminish the friction which arises from the use of heavy weights—these being in very large clocks almost incredibly heavy; for instance, the weights used by me for my clock in the Great International Exhibition of 1862 amounted to more than two tons. Whatever the cause of inequality of movement in the clock, whether it be dust or dirt, or insufficient oil, or whether it be wind delaying or expediting the progress of the hands on the dial, the remontoire regulates and counteracts.

THE DIALS.

The utility of a Public Clock is considerably enhanced by its being provided with a dial marking the time in the simplest and most unmistakeable lines, so that it may readily be ascertained at any reasonable distance from the clock-tower what is the hour either by day or night. In order that this important requisite may be attained, it is of course necessary that the dial shall be so constructed as to be visible both by night and day, and so arises the necessity for providing illuminating power either from within or from without. Now the simplest method, and perhaps also in the end the least objectionable,

is that followed at the Horse Guards, where the dial
forms part of the tower itself, and is lighted not from

Memorial Turret Clock Dial

within, but from without.   The advantage of this
arrangement is, that the architect can make the dial
harmonize with the character of the building, that
the illuminating power is kept apart from the
clock, and if the centre of the dial be slightly sunk
the hands may be brought quite close to the face, so
as to prevent any seeming error in time, as is sometimes caused by the convexity of a copper dial.   The
figures too, having been. once carefully divided and

cut into the stone, are renewed, so to speak, by
merely being painted over.

Dials may be made of any material, wood, stone,
slate, iron, brass, copper, and coloured or semi-opaque
glass. Copper dials possess many advantages, and
these have been of late years preferred, except where
more ornamental dials are required, in which case slate
and skeleton frames are used with good effect. The
large dial of my great clock which was placed over
the principal entrance of the International Exhibition
Building in the Cromwell Road was of slate, elabo-
rately enamelled with white and gold on a blue
ground. Another kind of dial having a good effect
is that erected by myself some time since for Sir
Moses Montefiore, at the Synagogue, Ramsgate,
consisting of a skeleton or framework of iron fitted
with Minton or encaustic tiles. A dial such as this
can thus be made with comparatively little expense
during the erection of the tower, and the architect
can then, as I have said, design it so as to be in
keeping with the edifice; the Minton tiles have also
the advantage of being almost indestructible, and
of being made of any pattern or colour. The chief
points to remember are that the dials should be slightly
sunk in the centre so as to allow the hour hand to
traverse in the sinking point close to the disc and the
figures, and especially that the dial should be made
large enough to distinctly show the hour. Properly

the dial should never be, less in diameter than one-tenth of the number of feet which it is distant from the ground, and in all cases where it is possible I should recommend it to be much larger than this. The dials of St Paul's and Westminster are larger than they would be under the above rule, and they are certainly not too large.   As to the colour of the dials, figures, and hands, there is not much choice ; dark ground and gilt figures, or white ground with black figures, or a skeleton frame with gilt figures are the chief in use.   In the white semi-transparent dials with opaque figures used for illuminated clocks, the time, which is seen with suffi-cient distinctness by night when the light is behind the figures, is not as clearly indicated by day.   To remedy this defect an invention has been applied by which the dial when illuminated at night throws out a beautiful transparent light admirably marking the position of the figures and hands, which being black or dark blue, or even strongly gilt, can also be distinctly seen by day, even as clearly as the long-approved copper dials painted black with gilt figures.

THE HANDS

should be most carefully made, and like the figures should be painted of a colour which shall most power-fully contrast with that of the dial.   The hands are almost invariably made of copper strengthened by diaphragms, and poised from the inside. In some old-fashioned clocks in which the hands have been poised from the outside the effect has been produced of a third hand, and numerous mistakes caused thereby. As to the shape of the hands, there is but one simple rule, namely, that the less of ornamentation in them the better. The minute hand should be perfectly plain, with a tapering but not too fine point, extending to the top of the figures; the hour hand should be of equal breadth and plainness, but its point should be more marked by perhaps an arrowhead or heart-shaped tip only reaching to the bottom of the figures. With large hands counterpoises are found necessary, and these should be placed inside the dial if possible, for they are when outside sometimes mistaken for the point of the hour hand. If a counterpoise must be placed outside, it is better to arrange that it shall be as little as possible, and that the inside counterpoise make up the difference, giving to the latter perhaps two thirds, and one third to the former,—but in any case care has to be taken to prevent the counterpoise appearing like a hand.

THE FRAME.

The old-fashioned clock-frame, known in the trade as the ' bedstead,' is now generally superseded by the horizontal frame originally introduced by the

French, which possesses the special advantage of not
only being durable and strong, but that it allows of
any part of the clock which may have been injured,
or may require cleaning, being easily taken out and
replaced without interfering with other portions of
the mechanism,—any wheel can be separately handled and removed.   In the old upright frame which is
even now still in use by some of the more ancient
firms of clock-makers, if any part of the clock be injured the entire machine must be taken to pieces.

THE FIXING

of a Turret Clock requires much careful forethought
and experienced labour; because whatever oversight
has been made by the architect in planning the clock-
room must be made good by the clock-maker who
has to fix up a public time-piece.   In the first place
the latter will take care that the supports of the clock
shall be sufficiently strong and free from vibration,
and that the movement shall be bolted securely to
the iron girders, or strong oak beams provided for the
purpose; he will remember that when it is intended
that the clock shall strike the hours and quarters, that
the bell or bells should be hung as high in the tower
as possible, so that when the stroke of the hammer
is given by a perfect fall of the weights, the louvres
of the tower should be so arranged as to bring out the

full sound of the bell, as in the case of the bell at St
Paul's cathedral, which, though only weighing 5 tons
4 cwts., is frequently heard on clear nights as far as
Windsor. He will in a word require to be acquainted with all the points of importance attached to his
rather intricate duty, or he may by failure render
nugatory the best workmanship that could be bestow-
ed in clock-making. The wiser arrangement as to
clock-fixing is to intrust the duty to the clock-maker,
and he will then necessarily bear the sole responsibility of any mistake.   '

THE WINDING and keeping in order is, as we
have said, a less laborious task as respects modern
clocks than those which were made fifty years
ago, inasmuch as, although it is the duty of a
clock-winder to watch daily the action of the time-
piece under his charge, he need not perform his
winding duties oftener than once a week. He must
be on the alert to observe any effect produced by
the action of the wind or the fall of snow upon
the hands of the clock, which under certain conditions is not uncommon; he must note by some
good regulator any tendency to variation in the
Church clock, and he must also observe the Equation
of Time, which is the difference between true and
mean solar time for each day, and which is not quite
the same for every year, because it moves on about a
quarter of a day in each year until leap year comes

and puts it back again. The Equation may be reckoned by an Equation Table, or by the time mentioned in the Almanacs as 'clock before' or 'clock after sun.' It is obviously a very important requisite for good time-keeping that good horological instruments shall be intrusted to skilful and careful hands. In many instances it has happened that escapements made upon the truest scientific principles, and set going in thorough working order, have been so injured by the mechanical genius of the village (some blundering sexton, or some jack-of-all-trades, whose education in mechanism must be exercised at the parish expense), that the new clock with all its merits has been seriously damaged. In such a case the clock-maker had better be at once consulted.

A MODERN TURRET CLOCK DESCRIBED.

The Turret Clock which the highest skill and the best experience of the value of the latest improvements can produce, may be thus described :—

The Bed or Frame is of cast-iron. The Barrel on which the cords are wound possesses a metal cap in front, and a ratchet or toothed wheel at the back end; between this cap and ratchet is a metal drum or tube adapted to the width of the Frame. Passing through the drum is an axle or barrel-arbor, on the back end of which the main or barrel-wheel is fitted

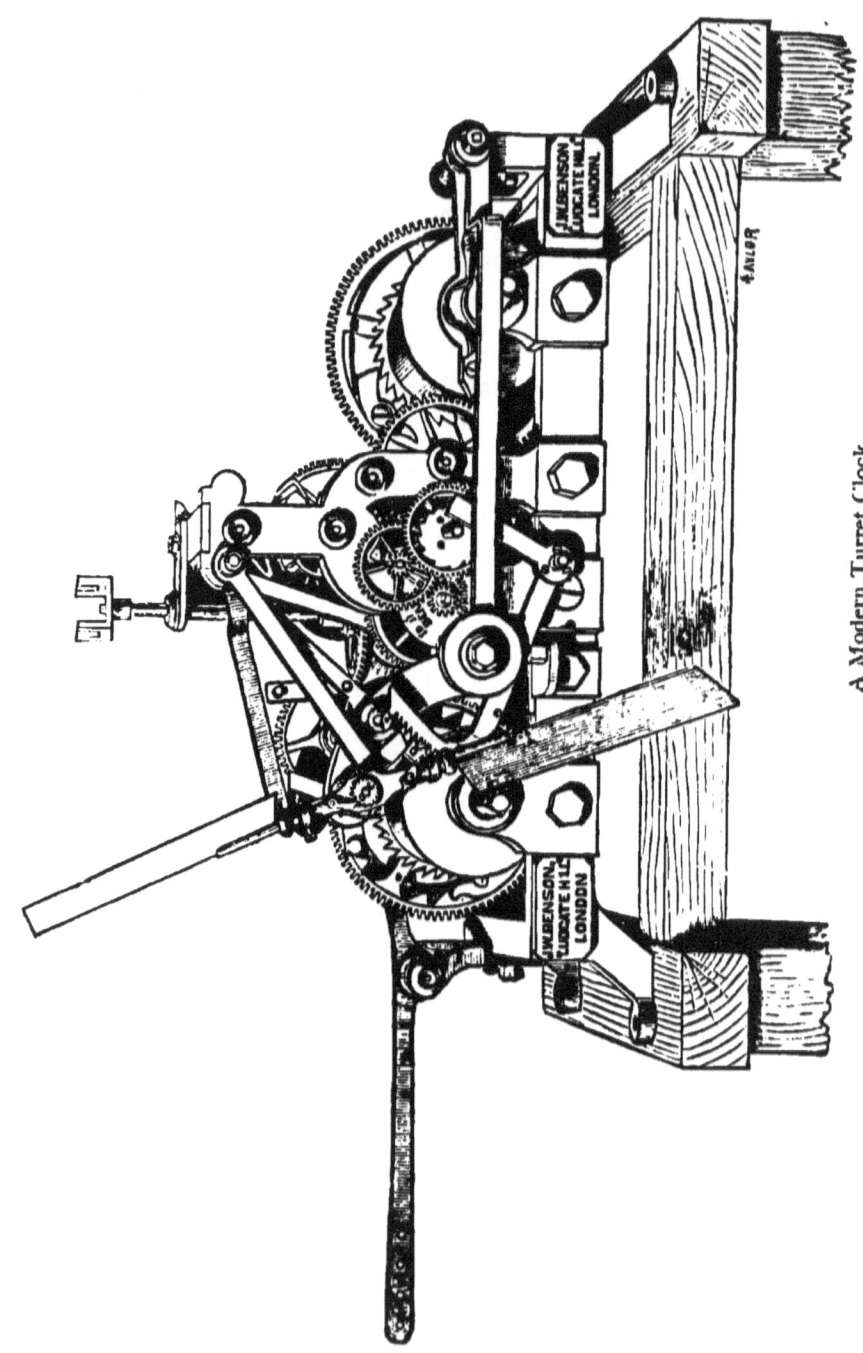

A Modern Turret Clock.

so as to allow the line which carries the weight to be
wound upon the barrel without moving the wheel,
which latter is kept in place by means of a cap or key
pinned tight on the arbor.   Upon the barrel wheels
are fitted clicks and springs, the former falling into
the toothed wheel or ratchet, and the latter keeping
the clicks in place while the clock is being wound up,
for as the weights are wound up the clicks prevent
the barrel running back.   At each end of the barrel-
arbor is a pivot in brass bearings fitted in plumber-
block, and bolted on the bed or frame with bolts and
washers.   Beyond the pivot on the front of the arbor
is a square to receive the winder.   The uprights or
small frames for carrying the going-train contain the
following; first, there is an arbor across the frame at
the back of which is a pinion working in the teeth
of the barrel-wheel; at the other end of the arbor is
the centre-wheel with teeth cut in it, and above this
wheel is another pinion running into it with a wheel
at the other end, termed the third wheel and pinion.
The escape-pinion runs into the third wheel; on this
arbor is fitted the escape-wheel, which has very fine
teeth cut in it.   Above the escape-wheel is an arbor
termed the verge arbor, to which are fitted the pallet
arms.   The pallet bits or pads working in the escape-
wheel teeth are of hardened steel polished.   At the
back end of the verge arbor is fitted the crutch which
connects the escapement and the pendulum rod.   The

escapement is that called the dead-beat or lever
escapement, found to be the best for time-keeping,
and least likely to get out of order. Upon the set-
hand arbor, used for setting the hands on the dial to
time, are two springs or keys to keep in place a wheel
fitted loosely on the arbor, and working in the teeth
of the centre-wheel. The hands are set by means of
the set key which fits on the end of the arbor in front.
At the back end of the same arbor is a joint by
means of which an iron rod connects the clock to the
dial, and works the outside hands. The whole of the
arbors are turned with suitable pivots into brass bearings screwed into the uprights, and all bolted to the
bed or frame by stout bolts and washers. On the
front upright is fitted an index or set-dial by which
to set the outside hands, and two wheels and pinions,
termed the motion or dial-work, fitted on sockets and
working on iron studs which are screwed into the

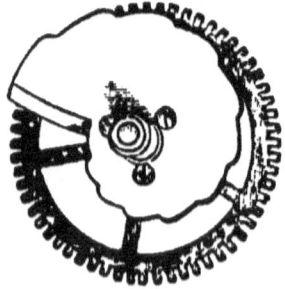

Hour-Wheel and Snail.

upright. Upon the largest
wheel, known as the hour-
wheel, is fixed a snail having
twelve steps in it for regulating the strokes to be given
at the different hours. The
striking-train consists of a
barrel similar to the going-
train, only that it has a camm or toothed-wheel
fitted on the back of the barrel-wheel for the pur-,

pose of raising the hammer which strikes the bell,
a lever being used called the hammer-tail.   This
barrel is fitted into bearings in plummer-block,
and bolted on frame.   The train of wheels and
pinions fitted in arbors, and working in brass bearings, consists of,—the pallet pinion fitted tight in the
pallet arbor and working in the teeth of the barrel-
wheel; at the front end of this arbor is a pallet of steel
working in the teeth of the rack (see next illustration),
and gathering it up as the blows of the hammer striking the hours are given on the barrel.   Above the
pallet arbor is a pinion running into the teeth of the
pallet wheel and termed the fly-pinion, as it is used for
regulating the blows or strokes.   Fans are attached to
the fly-pinion to assist in regulating the striking,—
the intervals between the strokes being thus made
longer or shorter as desired.   Fitted to the fly-frame is
a ratchet with two clicks and springs, these being used
to prevent the train being stopped too suddenly, and
the damage likely to arise therefrom.   At the right-
hand side of the clock frame is an arbor to carry the
work for the maintaining power, by means of which
work the clock is kept going even while it is being
wound up, and injury to the escapement is at the
same time prevented.   But for this maintaining
power during the winding-up, whilst the pendulum
is vibrating to and fro, the pallets are liable to catch
the teeth of the wheel, and these are so fine as to be

readily injured.   As properly fixed the clock cannot
be wound up unless this maintaining power is put in

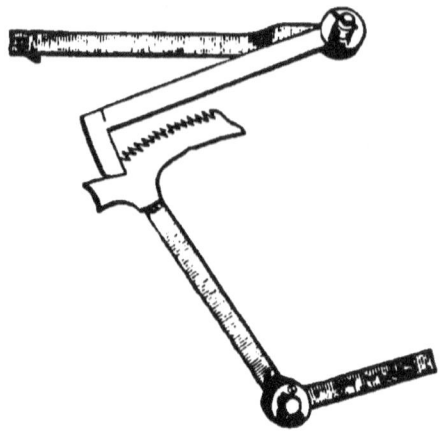

The Rack.

action by means of a lever passing in front of the
barrel-square, so that the winder cannot be put on
the square until the lever is raised and puts this power
in action.   The repeating work for the striking-train
is fitted on brass sockets working on wrought-iron
studs screwed into the front upright, and consists of
the Rack-hook, Warning, Locking, and Lifting
pieces.   The Rack is a portion of a circle with a
number of half-circular teeth cut on its edge ; at the
end of the Rack is the Rack-arm fitted with a spring
having a nib or pin in it, which nib or pin falls upon
the steps of the before-mentioned hour-snail, and thus
the different strokes are given at the hours; as the
nib falls nearer the centre the rack drops a greater

number of teeth.   The Rack-hook is placed above
the rack to catch the rack as it is gathered up by the
gathering pallets, and when the proper number of
strokes has been given this hook falls into a deep
tooth, and then, by means of a locking-piece attached
to it, causes the train to be locked with the stop-
piece on the fly-pinion arbor, this latter piece forming part of both the locking and warn-
ing work.   The lifting-piece lifts the
rack-hook out of the deep tooth in
the rack and locking, by means of a
snail or eccentric fitted on the set-
hand arbor.   On this lifting-piece is
also a piece for the warning, fitted on a
small stud.   The pendulum rod has a
brass top, and some adjusting work
with a steel suspension spring set in
brass, by means of which the clock
can be put in beat with great exact-
ness, there being no necessity with
this adjustment to bend the crutch as
heretofore, for the crutch on the verge
arbor has a pin screwed into it which
communicates the escapement to the
adjusting work or pendulum, and
keeps it in motion.   At the bottom
of the pendulum rod is an iron screw
and nut by means of which the pen-

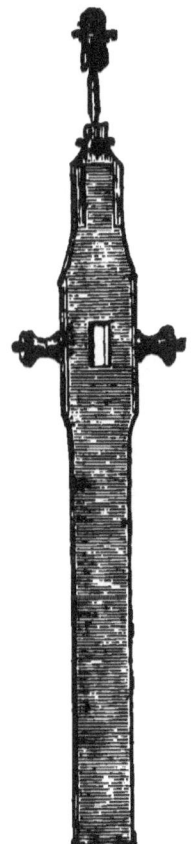

Pendulum Rod.

dulum bob is raised or lowered, and the clock made
to go faster or slower. The motion or dial work for
driving the hands are outside at the back of the
dials, and consist of two wheels and pinions working in one another, the larger of the two being fitted
to a socket and tube. At the other end of this
tube is another socket for the hour hand to be fixed
to ; and through this tube passes another iron rod, at
one end of which rod is fitted one of the pinions
and the minute hand, the other wheel and pinion
being fitted on a socket worked upon a stud in a
cock bolted on a bar called the dial bar. If the
clock has to drive more than one pair of dial hands,
wheels called bevelled or angle wheels are used,
which may be cut to suit any angle, so it will not
matter how far off the dials may be fitted, or how
many they may be, so long as the proper expansion
and universal joints are fitted to them. The Ham-
mer-work consists of an iron frame with an arbor
pivoted into brass bearings, and upon this arbor is
fitted a lever, one end of the lever holding the ham-
mer-head, and the other end raising the hammer.
The lifting of the hammer is done by means of a
wire from the hammer-tail previously mentioned.
There is also a steel spring attached to the lever to
prevent the hammer chattering on the bell.

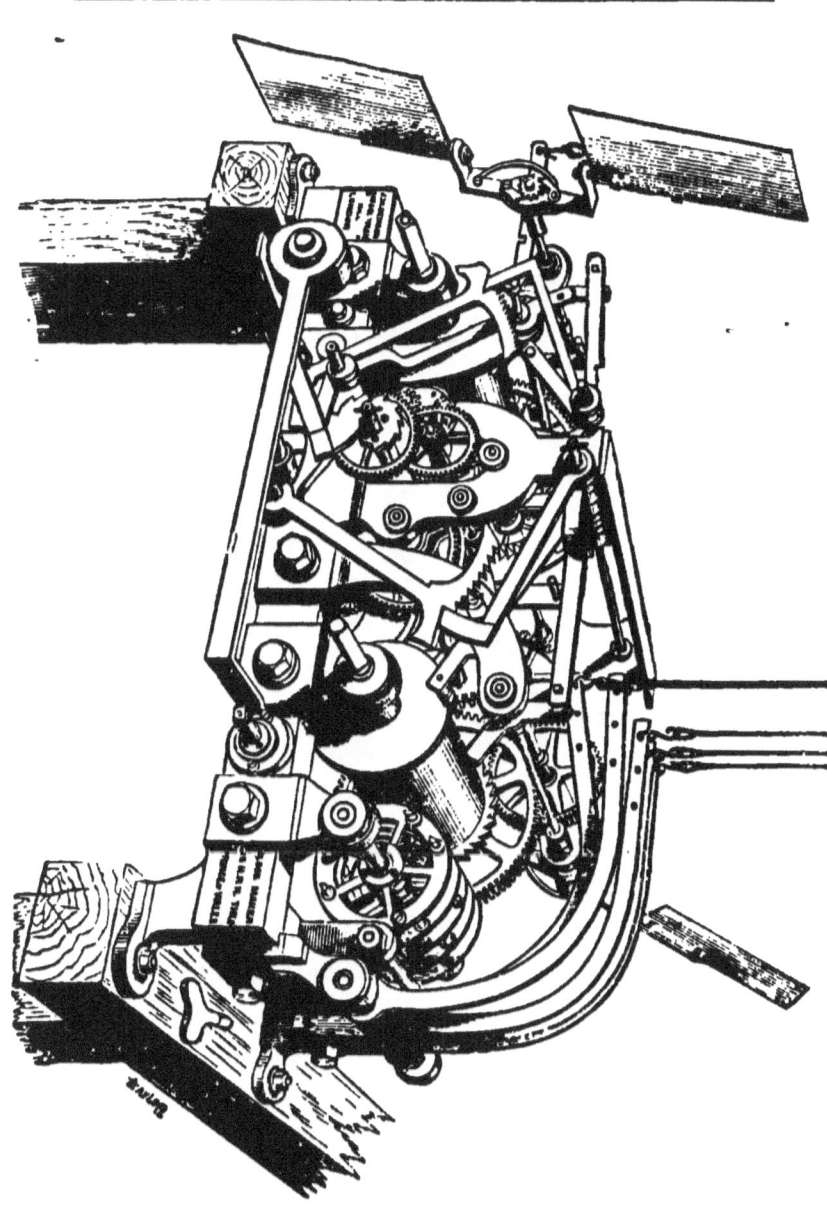

QUARTER or CHIME CLOCKS differ from the above only in having another barrel and train of wheels to provide the extra power for such striking and chiming.

GAS WHEEL FOR ILLUMINATED DIALS.

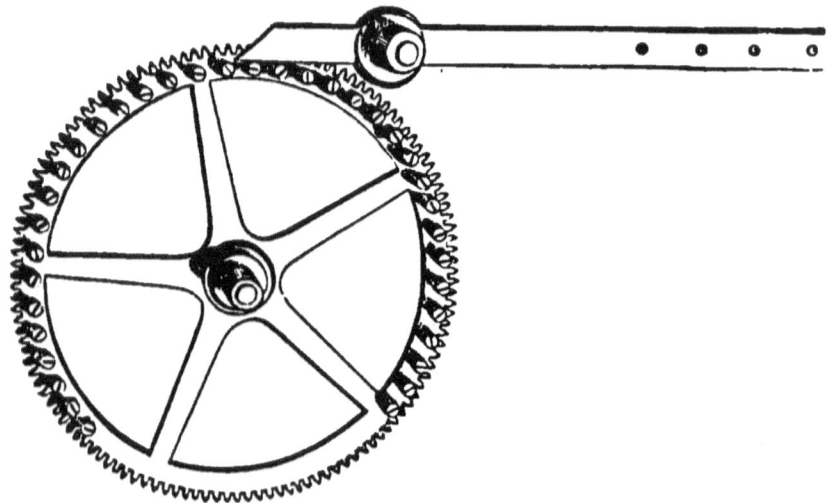

In instances where it is requisite that the clock face should be visible at a great distance, it is necessary that the dial should be made of semi-transparent glass and be illuminated by gas, which is usually turned as low as possible by day and turned on at night by means of the 24-hour wheel, as shown in the annexed illustration, the time for the turning on being regulated by the man in charge of the clock, who takes out or screws in the pins placed in the rim for that purpose.

NEST OF BEVELLED WHEELS FOR FOUR DIALS.

These wheels should be rather large, inasmuch as they have to carry the hands moving upon the face of the dial. The size of these wheels varies of course with the size of the clock, but they are seldom less than five inches and are generally from seven to nine inches wide.

HAMMER AND BELL.

The next engraving exhibits the relative positions of hammer and bell in a turret clock,—the hammer being fixed at right angles to the swing of the bell, so that the blow of the hammer should not drive the bell out of reach of its next blow, and this position least interfering with the ringing of the bell, when the bell is required to be rung. The hammer spring,

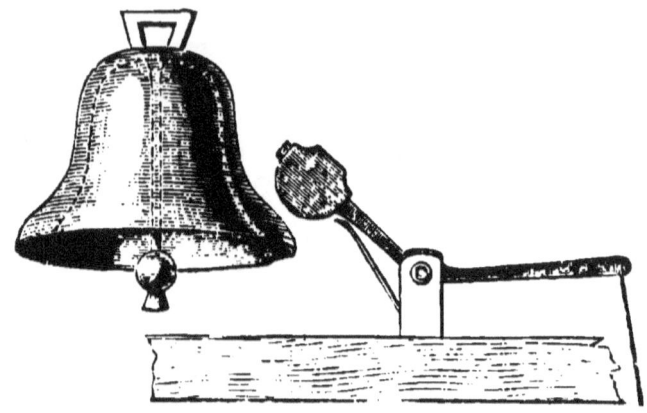

Hammer and Bell.

as shown, is sometimes so adjusted as to allow of the hammer being brought nearer or further from the bell.

THE GREAT CLOCKS OF THE INTERNATIONAL EXHIBITION OF 1862.

BENSON'S GREAT CLOCK.

The movement of this clock, next to that at Westminster, is the largest in the world, and, in point of quality of material and finish of workmanship, it is unequalled by any. The three main wheels are each two feet in diameter, and cast in the solid, of the very finest gun-metal, the teeth being afterwards cut by an engine made expressly for that purpose. The frame is of the best wrought-iron planed to a

Benson's Great Clock.—The Exterior.

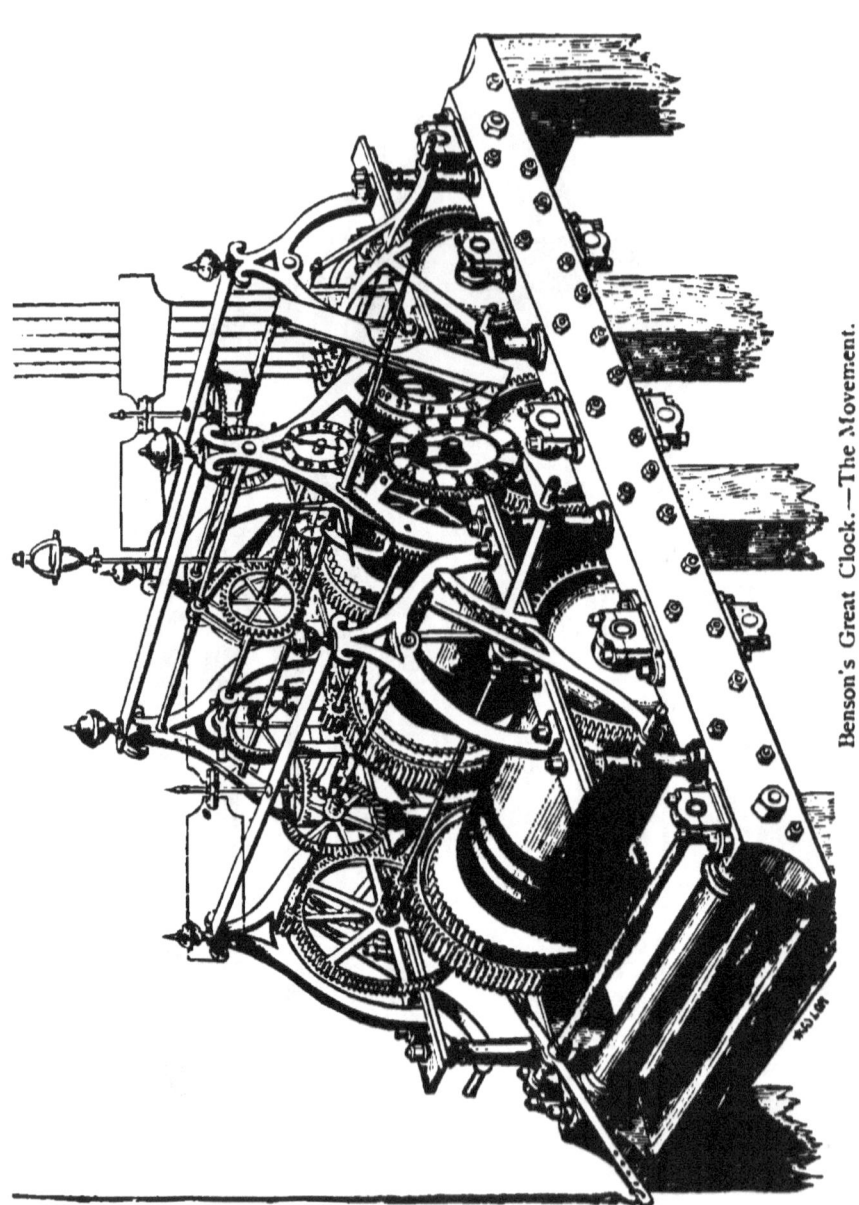

Benson's Great Clock.—The Movement.

smooth surface, and by means of a contrivance, known to engineers as plumber blocks, any part of the mechanism may be removed without disturbing the remainder. The pendulum, which is self-compensating, is over 15 feet long, and vibrates or beats once in two seconds. The quarter chimes, which are struck on four bells, are a modification of those of S. Mary, Cambridge.

The great weights necessary to drive so large a clock, and which by the friction they would cause might prejudicially influence its performance, are in this case not allowed to act directly upon the pendulum, but are made to wind up a small auxiliary weight once every half-minute, and this weight imparts an exactly uniform impulse to the pendulum at each vibration. This arrangement, which is called the *remontoir*, is supplemented in this clock by a double lever escapement of a novel kind, in connection with that known as Graham's Dead Beat.

A CALENDAR AND WIND-DIAL

are useful additions to some edifices. The CALENDAR indicates on special circles of a large dial—by means of three separate hands—the month of the year, the day of the month, and the day of the week. The peculiarity of this invention is that it needs no correction for the long and short months, nor even for the month of February, with its occasional 29 days;

12

as by means of a wheel cut for the successive months
in a period of four years, and which takes that
time for a single revolution, the calendar is rendered
a perpetual one. The mechanism which directs the
pointers to the days of the week and of the month is
discharged, by the clock, each night at 12 o'clock,
when the levers shift the hands to their proper places
on their several dials. On the first of the month all
three hands on the dial are moved at the same
instant.

The WIND-DIAL is lettered with the four cardinal
points of the compass and the 12 intermediates. The
hand which points on the dial is connected by rods
and bevelled wheels with a vane at the top of the
house, placed 20 feet above the roof in order to be
affected, not by wind eddies, but by the true current
of air. The connecting rods boxed in the wall are
broken at every eight feet with universal joints, and
hardened steel is used for all pivots and sockets. The
dials are generally made of semi-transparent ground
glass and are lit by gas after dark. In a set of Clock
Calendars which I some time since provided for His
Grace the Duke of Portland, the clock showed the
time on four illuminated dials five feet nine inches in
diameter, chiming quarters, hours, &c. (the well-
known Cambridge chimes) on bells of 12 cwt., repeating the hour after the 1st, 2nd, and 3rd quarters. The
two sides of an adjoining tower show a calendar

similar to the one above mentioned, with the addition
of an extra circle on the dial to mark the age of the
moon and the equation of time, so that each dial has
four circles, besides the circle of the moon, shifted
simultaneously at 12 o'clock every night

SUN-DIALS

(see illustration on following page) are chiefly used
now to mark the solar meridian or noon.   Those
which indicate other hours have a gnomon with
its edge parallel to the earth's axis and inclined to
the horizon at the angle corresponding to the latitude
of the place in which the dial is fixed.

CARILLON CHIMES.

These beautiful examples of al fresco music, which
have been hithertoc hiefly identified with Belgium, are
now being produced in England with perhaps even
more pleasing and satisfactory musical effect.   Caril-
lons attached to Church or Turret Clocks are being
set up in various churches and mansions in different
parts of the kingdom, and it is not improbable that
the taste for such chimes may grow with the opportunity for hearing them.   As in musical clocks, the
works for time-keeping and those for chiming are
entirely distinct, with the exception of the means by
which the clock at certain fixed intervals lets off the

chiming machinery after the striking is done.   Chimes
were much more popular years ago than they have

J.W.BENSON
58&60 LUDGATE HILL
LONDON.

Sun-Dial.

been until lately.   The old-fashioned machinery used
to be rude enough, consisting chiefly of a large wooden
barrel, stuck, like that of a musical box, with pins.
These pins pulled the hammers that struck upon the
bells, and the time was regulated by a rope coiled

round one end of the barrel driving two or three
wheels connected with a fly-wheel.   More recent inventions have improved upon these conditions.   The
barrel is sometimes of cast-iron instead of wood, with
steel or brass pins fixed in it to lift the hammers, and
a very heavy weight is necessary to give the motive
power.   Instead of the ordinary method of raising the
hammers and letting them fall by means of the pins
on a chime barrel, the hammers are immediately after
use returned to their places in striking position ready
to be liberated by the pins on the chime barrel, and
upon being so liberated are prepared to strike again.
The tunes to be played upon these bells will of course
be such as are adapted to the particular number of
bells in each case, and the cost of the entire chimes
depends upon the number and sizes of the bells so
used,—varying with the circumstances,—the size and
capacity of the tower, and the difficulties to be overcome in providing accommodation for the necessary
bells, weights, chime barrel, &c.   In each instance, as
with turret clocks, the cost of the whole works depends to a great extent upon the cost of fixing the
machinery.   The tones of the bells have to be carefully provided for, as also the best position in which
they can be heard at a distance.   With fourteen bells
of different sizes almost any tune can be played.

One was erected recently upon the new principle,
of which the cost was something under £5000,

including 12 bells weighing from five to seven cwt.
each, clock, architect's charges, gas-fitting, and £1200
for timber-trussing, floors, &c. The Carillon machine
is let off by the clock and plays seven times on the
ringing peal of bells, but is adapted to play twenty-
eight tunes on fifteen bells. It is wound up every
morning and plays eight times in twenty-four hours,
i. e. once every three hours, giving the tune on each
occasion three times, and occupying about four
minutes in doing so. At the expiration of the 24
hours the tune changes involuntarily, and of course
with seven tunes there is one for each day in the
week. The Carillon machinery is connected with the
clock and set in motion thereby, by a lever which at
three hours' intervals dislodges a pin and allows the
weights, 14 cwt. each, to act upon the machinery, the
speed being easily regulated, as in clock-work, by revolving vanes. The barrels are five feet long, by one
foot in diameter, and are studded with brass pins like
that of a musical box. When the bells are required
to be rung, a bar is turned down on the keys which
prevents the motion of the machinery for any length
of time that the ringing is to be continued. Not-
withstanding that the twenty-six hammers weigh from
2 cwt. to 70lbs each, it is possible that the tunes could
be played by means of an ivory keyboard, as in a
church organ, and with almost as much ease and
facility.

Persons requiring to know the cost of a Church or Turret Clock should furnish the Clockmaker with the following data :— .

How many Dials?	
Their Diameter?	
Their Elevation, or distance from the ground?	
If to be Illuminated?	
Of what material is Dial to be?	
Can the Movement be placed on a level with the centre of Dial, if not, how far above or below it?	
Is the Clock to strike? if so, on what size or weight bell?	
If to strike half-hours or quarters, or how many bells, and their sizes and weights?	
What number of feet can be obtained for descent of weights?	
What length of Pendulum will the building admit of, and is a compensating Pendulum required?	

A FEW DATES AND DETAILS FOR
ALMANAC READERS.

THE following data may be found useful in studying an Almanac.

The columns for SUNRISE AND SUNSET are nearly the same year after year for any given place; for by the alteration of styles and the day allowed at Leap Year the civil and astronomical year are almost exactly the same; but the difference in latitude of different places makes a London almanac useless for sunrise and sunset, say at Edinburgh. The sun rises at each place to a greater height in June than in December, but he is always at a less height in Edinburgh than in London both in winter and summer, Edinburgh being farther than London from the equator, where the sun is more immediately overhead.

The RISING AND SETTING OF THE MOON vary greatly day by day. The moon is constantly moving eastward, and she is not moving in the same path with the sun; the latitude and longitude of the observer's position, the place of the moon in her orbit, the rapidity of her motion, and other particulars, are to be taken into account in computing her rising and setting.

The GOLDEN NUMBER is a term arising from the discovery that the sun performs his annual course 19 times to the moon's 235. The golden number is the

number which any given year holds in the Lunar
Cycle. After the lapse of 19 years the new moons
occur on the same days of the same months as before.
This discovery being esteemed by the Romans to be
highly important, they set up the rule for ascertaining
the number of the year in the Lunar Cycle in a tab-
let with letters of gold, hence the term Golden
Number. To find the year of the Lunar Cycle add
one to the present year, then divide by 19 and the
remainder will show the year of the Cycle.

The EPACT is the number of days which must be
added to a lunar year to complete a solar year.
Twelve lunar months being nearly 11 days less than
the solar year, the new moons in one year falling 11
days earlier than in the year preceding it, it becomes
necessary on the fourth year, when the difference
would amount to 33 days, to take off 30 days as an
intercalary month, during which the moon has made
a revolution, and the three remaining would be the
epact or 'addition,' which thus continues to vary
until the 19 years have expired, and the new moons
recur as before.

The SOLAR CYCLE is complete in 28 years, after
which the days of the month return to the same days
of the week as before.

The DOMINICAL OR SUNDAY LETTER, as one of
the first seven letters of the alphabet, used to denote
the days of the week, one of which must of course

fall on the Sunday throughout the year. Owing to
Leap Year their order every fourth year is disturbed,
so that the Solar Cycle must pass round before the
letters can fall to the same days of the week.

THE NUMBER OF DIRECTION. The Council of
Nice having decided, A.D. 325, that Easter Day is
always the first Sunday after the full moon which
happens upon or next after the 21st of March, it follows that Easter Day cannot take place earlier than
the 22nd of March, or later than the 25th of April.
The number of Direction is that day of the 35, on
which Easter Sunday falls.

ROMAN INDICTION was a period of fifteen years,
appointed by the Emperor Constantine, A.D. 312, for
the payment of certain taxes. It was observed by
the Greek and Roman Churches.

THE JULIAN PERIOD consists of 7980 years, produced by the multiplication into each other of the
Solar and Lunar Cycles and the Roman Indiction,
$28 \times 19 \times 15 = 7980$. This period is reckoned from
709 before the Creation of the World, when the three
Cycles are supposed to have commenced together;
the lapse of the entire period will be A.D. 3267.

EQUATION OF TIME is the difference between the
time as indicated by a sun-dial, and that by a good
clock. It is necessary because the sun, the chief
agent in measuring time, does not upon all days
of the year appear to move equally fast, inasmuch as

an hour by a sun-dial, correctly indicating the sun's motion, is sometimes longer, sometimes shorter, than an hour by the clock, the hours of which are supposed to be perfectly equal, although the sun's are not. The Equation of Time shows how many minutes are to be added to, or subtracted from, sun-dial time in order to show clock time. The same table of equation will serve all over the world. [See following pages for Equation Table.]

TRUE OR SOLAR TIME is that marked by the sun, and it is taken at the moment when he has attained his greatest height above the horizon,—such a moment being of course dependent upon the latitude of the place of observation. The solar time by which our nautical standard is fixed, is that of the meridian of Greenwich.

SIDEREAL TIME is that measured by the fixed stars, which are at such an immense distance from the earth that the diurnal motion of the earth brings these stars to the meridian at sufficiently regular intervals. It is necessary, however, to remember when making observations for sidereal time that these must be made from fixed or twinkling stars, not from planets.

Of the various Eras from which time has been dated, the following are the chief:—

A.M. *Anno Mundi.* The Year of the
World, dating from the Creation, according to Jewish Calendar .. *5635*

The Deluge, Era of, variously
reckoned   ..   ..   **2348 to 3155** B.C.
The first Olympiad   ..   ..   .. **776** B.C.
A.U.C. or *Anno Urbis Conditæ*, the year
of the building of Rome ..   .. **753** B.C.
The Hegira, or Flight of Mahomet from
Mecca to Medina ..   ..   .. **622** A.D.
The Birth of Christ in the year of the
World **4004**
The Jewish year 5635 commenced Sept.
12, 1874 A.D.

A TABLE OF THE EQUATION OF TIME,
For regulating Clocks and Watches for 1875.

Day	January		February		March		April		May		June	
1	3m.fa.45s.		13m.fa.50s.		12m.fa.36s.		4m.fa. 1s.		3m. sl. 0s.		2m. sl. 30s.	
3	4	41	14	4	12	11	3	25	3	14	2	12
5	5	36	14	16	11	45	2	49	3	26	1	51
7	6	29	14	24	11	16	2	14	3	35	1	30
9	7	20	14	29	10	47	1	41	3	43	1	7
11	8	9	14	30	10	16	1	8	3	48	0	44
13	8	55	14	29	9	43	0	36	3	51	0	19
15	9	39	14	24	9	9	0	5	3	51	0 fa.	6
17	10	20	14	16	8	35	0 sl.	24	3	50	0	31
19	10	58	14	6	7	59	0	52	3	46	0	57
21	11	33	13	53	7	23	1	18	3	40	1	23
23	12	5	13	37	6	46	1	42	3	32	1	48
25	12	34	13	19	6	9	2	5	3	22	2	14
27	13	0	12	58	5	32	2	25	3	10	2	39
29	13	22	- - -		4	55	2	44	2	55	3	4
31	13	41	- - -		4	19	- - -		2	39	- - -	

EQUATION OF TIME TABLE, 1875—*continued.*

Day	July		August		September		October		November		December	
1	3m. fa. 28s.		6m. fa. 5s.		0m. sl. 3s.		10m.sl.16s.		16m.sl.18s.		10m.sl.52s.	
3	3	51	5	57	0	41	10	54	16	19	10	5
5	4	13	5	47	1	20	11	30	16	17	9	17
7	4	33	5	34	2	0	12	5	16	12	8	26
9	4	52	5	19	2	41	12	38	16	4	7	33
11	5	9	5	2	3	22	13	10	15	52	6	38
13	5	24	4	42	4	4	13	40	15	37	5	42
15	5	38	4	20	4	47	14	8	15	18	4	45
17	5	49	3	55	5	29	14	33	14	56	3	47
19	5	59	3	29	6	12	14	56	14	31	2	47
21	6	6	3	1	6	54	15	17	14	2	1	48
23	6	11	2	31	7	36	15	34	13	30	0	48
25	6	13	1	59	8	17	15	49	12	55	0 fa.	12
27	6	14	1	26	8	58	16	1	12	17	1	12
29	6	12	0	52	9	37	16	10	11	36	2	11
31	6	8	0	16	·	· ·	16	16	·	· ·	3	10

Note.—Fa. means clock to be fast, *that is,* your Clock, to be right, must be so much faster than the Sun-Dial—Sl. that your Clock must be so much slower than the Sun-Dial.

To set a Clock or Watch on any Day by means of this Table:—Take out the number of Minutes and Seconds which stand against that day, and make your Clock or Watch so much faster or slower (according as the table is marked *fa.* or *sl.*) than the time on a good Sun-Dial. Thus, on January 1st, the Clock must be set 3m. 45s. *faster* or *before* the Dial ; on the 1st of October, it must be set 10m. 16s. *slower.* Correct the Watch when the Dial marks just an hour, as 9, 10, 11, 1, 2, 3, or 4 o'clock. Noon is *not* best, nor near Sunrise or Sunset.